"Are you really innocent, Rachel?"

She nodded, half-ashamed to have to confess her lack of experience.

"Rare in this day and age," Cass commented wonderingly. "But you're not frigid." Rachel blushed as she recalled her surrender in his arms. "Sooner or later you'll take the plunge. Perhaps you've a husband in view and are keeping yourself for him."

"Actually I haven't, but I've always considered casual lovemaking rather cheap," she said primly.

"I see," he drawled. "But perhaps you could be persuaded to change your mind."

Rachel drew a deep breath. He was playing with her, but it was not a game she enjoyed. She feared he was regarding her only as an attractive diversion....

Other titles by
ELIZABETH ASHTON
IN HARLEQUIN ROMANCES

Other titles by
ELIZABETH ASHTON
IN HARLEQUIN PRESENTS

Many of these titles are available at your local bookseller
or through the Harlequin Reader Service.

For a free catalogue listing all available Harlequin Romances,
send your name and address to:

HARLEQUIN READER SERVICE,
M.P.O. Box 707, Niagara Falls, N.Y. 14302
Canadian address: Stratford, Ontario, Canada N5A 6W2

or use coupon at back of book.

The Garden of the Gods

by

ELIZABETH ASHTON

Harlequin Books

TORONTO • LONDON • NEW YORK • AMSTERDAM
SYDNEY • HAMBURG • PARIS

Original hardcover edition published in 1978
by Mills & Boon Limited

ISBN 0-373-02256-5

Harlequin edition published April 1979

CHAPTER ONE

CLOUD wrack scudding across the sky parted intermittently to allow moonlight to pour down upon the deck of the caique. In one of these intervals the prone figure on the boards was illuminated in a silver flood. Wraith-pale in her revealing white swimsuit, she looked like a marble statue and her long wet hair clung about her neck and shoulders like seaweed. The man beside her stood stock still staring down at her as if he was seeing a ghost, his handsome mouth drawn in at the corners as if he had swallowed a bitter draught. When he had thrown the lifebelt into the sea and jumped in after it to pull out the foolhardy swimmer, he had had no premonition that he would be confronted by a spectre from his past. Even during the process of resuscitation he had not noticed the likeness in the fitful light. Now the unveiled moon revealed every detail.

The Greek boy standing beside him holding the blanket he had bade him fetch from the cabin mistook the reason for his immobility. Anxiously he touched his arm.

'*Kyrie*, is she dead?'

For that would explain the look of desperation on his face. To have dared so much and be cheated in the end was hard luck.

Cass Dakers seemed to revive from the trance that had momentarily enwrapped him. He passed his hand over his brow as if to wipe away the unwelcome memories and took the blanket, wrapping it around the inert figure at his feet.

'No, she is not dead, Dion,' he said in Greek. 'Merely completely exhausted by her swim.' He knelt beside her and felt the girl's pulse. 'She'll recover consciousness in a few moments.'

'Saint Spyridon had her in his keeping,' Dion declared simply, for the Corfiotes believed implicitly in the guardianship of their patron saint. If we had not picked her up the current would have carried her across to Albania with this wind and at this time of night it runs fast. The Saint guided us to save her.'

He glanced fearfully at the dimly seen shapes of the mountains across the strait. Albania, the forbidden land, from whence strangers had difficulty in extricating themselves. It was almost a miracle that Cass had spotted the lone swimmer, and he would not have done so if the moon had not for a moment sent a silver shaft across the sea. Even so he had not been sure it was not a porpoise, until he had seen the shine of her hair through his spyglass.

'I doubt she would have made the shore,' Cass said grimly. 'She was just about all in when I reached her.'

He picked up from the deck a packet wrapped in oilskin which he had detached from the strings that bound it between the girl's shoulders.

'This may tell us who she is,' he remarked, and found himself oddly reluctant to make that discovery. Who could it be who had come to him out of the sea with that unforgettable face and figure, which for years he had sought to banish entirely from his mind?

'*Kyrie*, you are wet.'

Dion handed him a towel which he draped over his broad shoulders; he was naked but for his soaking shorts. He had cast off his sweater and shoes when he had plunged into the sea in the wake of the lifebelt to which the girl was clinging with the last of her strength. He was surprised to discover that he was shivering, as he mechanically rubbed his shoulders while he stared at the figure at his feet. Surely very few women had hair like that, silver shot with gold? But by now she would be much older than this girl, middle-aged in fact, and his imagination stimulated by the silver gilt hair was creating fantasies. The moon playing peep-bo in the sky was again obscured as he pulled on his sweater. The girl was a stranger and that affair was over long time ago, but he was dismayed at the resurgence of memory, for he believed he had eradicated completely all recollections of his youthful folly.

The old man in the stern, the only other member of the crew and the owner of the boat, called to the youth to take the tiller and came stumping across the deck towards the flotsam they had rescued. At that moment the moon shone out again, released from its veiling clouds, to illuminate the girl's pale face above the blanket framed in her long hair, blanched to ivory by its rays. He crossed himself fervently.

'She is a nereid, *Kyrie*,' he exclaimed. 'She'll bring bad luck. You had better put her back into the sea.'

'She felt too substantial to be a sea nymph,' Cass returned. He did not laugh at the old Corfiote's suggestion, knowing how superstitious the Islanders were. That was partly why he was there, to study their myths and folklore. Though officially a Christian, old Yanni believed firmly in nature spirits.

'That was her cunning,' he declared stoutly. 'Nereids bring no good to mortal men. Drop her overboard.'

A loud protest came from the stern. *'Kyrie! Ochi!'*

Yanni threw an anxious glance towards his grandson.

'She has put a spell upon Dion already,' he declared. 'And he betrothed to a girl with a whole vineyard for her dowry! Get rid of her, *Kyrie*, before she bewitches you also.'

Cass Dakers laughed scornfully.

'I'm proof against any female wiles,' he returned, 'but this poor soul is too far gone to endanger any of us. I'll put her in the cabin, she'll be warmer there.'

He stooped and picked up the blanket-shrouded form in his strong arms. Her long hair hung over his arm like silver rain and Yanni again crossed himself.

'That hair is not natural,' he persisted.

'Heaps of Nordic girls have hair like that,' Cass told him, as much to convince himself as his listener. 'She had papers with her—your mermaids don't carry their credentials around with them. We shall soon discover she is a perfectly ordinary human mortal. Hand me that packet.'

Yanni picked up the oilskin envelope rather as if he expected to find it red-hot and handed it to the Englishman. He looked unconvinced and was careful not to touch the blanket. Cass carried the girl into the tiny cabin and laid her down on the single bunk. An evil-smelling oil lantern hung from the low ceiling and by the light of it he examined the contents of packet.

They consisted of a book of travellers' cheques, a passport and some drachma notes. From the second he learned that this waif from the sea was called Rachel Reed, her status disguised by the modern Ms, she was a British subject, of medium height and London-born, twenty years ago. That was all. He stared at the almost unrecognisable photograph, which was so oddly familiar. He did not know the name, was unacquainted with any Reeds. Evidently her presence in the sea was premeditated. She would not have secured her money and passport with such care if she had not intended to use them. She must have hoped to reach Corfu, for it was inconceivable that she would want to land in Albania. The strait at the northern part of the island was narrow, about two miles wide, and Corfu only about a mile from the point where she had been picked up. Not an impossible feat for a strong swimmer if it had not been for the treacherous currents of which she had probably been unaware. She must have been aboard some yacht or liner, and he recalled vaguely a white shape travelling swiftly southwards. But what could have happened to cause her to risk her life in the sea?

Cass shrugged his shoulders and rewrapped the money and passport in the oilskin. He had no wish to pry into her affairs more than was necessary. He had come out with Yanni and his grandson for the experience of a trip which was not quite as innocent as fishing. Though Albania was a closed country, a certain amount of smuggling went on, and Cass was intrigued by its possibilities. There was not much risk of interception and being a writer he scented copy, but he had certainly not bargained on picking up a mysterious female upon the return journey. He suspected Yanni's desire to be rid of their unwelcome visitor was prompted by more practical motives than superstition; he did not want a witness of his nocturnal adventures. Himself, the natives trusted; he had lived among them long enough for them to know he did not talk about their doings. What he wrote in his books did not trouble them, and it was unlikely the Customs officials read them.

Well, Rachel Reed was too far gone to take heed of what cargo or lack of cargo the boat carried, but when they came ashore she would revive and perhaps Yanni feared she might ask awkward questions. It seemed he would have no option but to accommodate her in his own house. Not that the villagers in the small community grouped below his residence were lacking in hospitality, they could not do too much for a stranger, but their cottages were very primitive, mostly comprising only two or three rooms with no space for a guest. It was an isolated spot and she probably did not know any Greek, while they knew no English beyond an odd word or two.

Cass sighed. Feminine complications were the last thing he wanted in his hermitage on the slopes of Mount Pantokrator, but it would not be for long. As soon as she was recovered she would go on her way to wherever it was she wanted to go and he could forget the incident.

Cass Dakers lived alone in his eyrie up on the cliff above the fishing hamlet. He employed no servant, being competent to cook and clean for himself. Often he was away all day, exploring remote corners of the island where the encroaching tourist invasion had not yet penetrated. He had left his car parked on the waterfront when he had come aboard Yanni's caique. Though he had decided he must give hospitality to this most unwelcome guest, he did not want her presence broadcast. He did not care for his reputation, but he very much disliked distorted paragraphs in the gossip columns about his private life, for he was sufficiently famous to be considered news. Corfu was his refuge from publicity and his address was known only to his publishers, his bank and the television company for which he did an occasional series about the animal and marine life of the Ionian Islands.

The girl on the bunk moved restlessly, throwing back the blanket. Her eyelids flickered, and opened, her bemused gaze focussed on the lantern.

'Where am I?'

The words were a husky whisper and there was fear in her wide eyes which looked dark in the dim light. Against his will Cass was moved by her plight. She looked so pathetically frail and vulnerable. He knelt down beside the bunk, and impulsively put a consoling arm around her shoulders. She raised herself a little to free herself from the coarse blanket and her flesh was soft and smooth to his touch.

'Don't worry,' he said reassuringly. 'You're safe and among friends. Go back to sleep.'

Rather to his dismay, she snuggled against him, her lips parting in a sweet smile.

'Daddy!' she murmured, and closed her eyes again.

She thought he was her father, and it was a relief to learn that she had someone who could be approached to succour her if she needed help. But Cass was feeling anything but paternal himself. The girl's slight body enclosed by his arm was stirring sleeping emotions, the result of having been too long without a woman. This one was likely to prove to be a damned nuisance, he reflected wryly, in more ways than one. He came to Corfu to work in peace away from the racket of London to which he had to return from time to time, where he was pursued by amorous women whom he took lightheartedly and discharged almost immediately when his urges were assuaged. He did not want a permanent tie with any one of them, for he despised women even when making use of them, and while he was immersed in a book he liked to be free of emotional distraction. This girl was more than tiresome, she was a menace.

She had sunk into a deep sleep of utter exhaustion and he laid her back on the bunk, drawing the blanket up over her shoulders, and went back on deck.

As the caique approached the shore, a dark shape gliding over dark water, for the moon had set, and dawn was only a grey gleam on the eastern horizon, he said to the crew:

'No word of this to anyone, if you please. Why and wherefore the *thespoinis* came to be in the sea I've yet to discover, but she would not want her presence gossiped about, I'm sure. Tomorrow I'll take her to the British Consulate in Corfu and that'll be the end of it. You, Yanni, have reasons for not wanting this expedition talked about. So muzzle your grandson and forget you ever saw her.'

Yanni indicated that he would only be too pleased to do so and sharply bade Dion hold his tongue. The lad was looking wistfully towards the cabin. Evidently he had been fascinated by the girl's beauty, so different from that of the dark-haired sturdy maidens with whom he was familiar.

'I would not say anything to harm the *thespoinis*,' he said earnestly.

Cass grinned sardonically, fully aware of the young man's feelings. The sooner Rachel Reed was despatched to Corfu the better for all concerned.

The village was still wrapped in slumber when the boat grounded. Not a light showed anywhere, though as soon as the light had broadened the fisherfolk would be astir. Cass carried his burden ashore and stowed it in the back of his car. The girl was so utterly spent she did not stir as he laid her on the rear seat. He closed the car door upon her and turned to pay Yanni his due. The old man looked worried and he told him earnestly :

'Be wary, *kyrie*, do not let her enchant you, but ...' his tone brightened, 'she may vanish in the daylight.'

Cass laughed shortly.

'I'm afraid that won't happen—I only wish it would!'

Rachel did not wake until about noon the following day. She had been too utterly worn out to be aware of what was happening to her. She had no clear recollection of anything after glimpsing the caique as she neared the end of her strength and with a last desperate effort to save herself had grasped the lifebelt thrown to her.

She discovered that she was in bed in a strange room. The shutters were closed against the midday heat and the muted light showed her plain whitewashed walls and a few pieces of furniture in dark wood. There was a strip of matting on the polished floor by the bed and she was covered by a duvet, the original continental quilt in a plain white cover. Her surroundings were austere to the point of primitiveness and she knitted her brows in the effort to recall how she came to be there. Someone, possibly the man who had thrown her the lifebelt and afterwards swum to her rescue, had brought her ashore and she was lodged in somebody's house, though it might be a Greek taverna. She became aware that she was enveloped in a man's white shirt, and recollecting the precious packet that contained all she possessed in the world, she fumbled desperately at her back, to find it was gone. She looked wildly round the room, but there was no sign of it, nor of her swim-suit; whoever had stripped her and put her to bed must have taken it. She could only hope the person was honest. As for the reason that had caused her pre-cipitous flight, she did not want to dwell upon it, it was something she wanted to forget and hoped would fade, as a nightmare fades with the coming of the morning light.

Panos Simonides, that gross creature, was a night-mare being, with his mat of thick curls above his low forehead and heavy pendulous face, like that of a bull without horns. As if she could ever ... She clutched her covering, shaken with a return of the fear and loath-ing which had driven her to take such a hazardous means of escape. She had been incredibly naïve and trusting, but a girl did not expect betrayal from her nearest and dearest. A feeling of desolation swept over her; no longer near, no longer dear but her worst enemy. She had only her own wit and resolution to depend upon now. She prayed that Panos would believe that she had perished in the sea, as she so nearly had done. If she could stay in hiding for a few days, he would be-come convinced of it when no body was washed ashore and nobody admitted to having rescued her. He would not linger long, for he was bound for Athens where his concerns needed his presence. Once he was on his way, she could go to Corfu and take a flight back to England where she could lose herself in the anonymity of Lon-don. But she could only do that if she recovered her money and passport, without which she was helpless; she had not even clothes to cover her.

A knock on the door cut short her meditations. With-out the knocker waiting for permission to enter, it was pushed open and a man came into her room. Rachel,

who had expected to see a Greek village woman, stared
at him blankly, dragging the duvet up to her chin. He
might have been Greek with his straight nose and
rounded chin, but the eyes were not Greek. Almond-
shaped, set slightly aslant under tilted brows, they were
a surprising light grey in contrast with his deeply tanned skin. Above medium height, he moved towards her
with feline grace, and there was an assurance about
him that spoke of maturity and success, emphasised by
the arrogant way he held his head. He wore a bright
blue tee-shirt over denim pants and when he spoke it
was in unaccented English.

'So you're awake at last.' His voice was pleasant and
deep. 'None the worse for your adventure, I hope?'

His eyes slid critically over her pale face, the tangled
mass of silver-gilt hair pouring over her shoulders and
her slim arms clutching the quilt, arms which had not
yet been touched by the Mediterranean sun, and
were pearly white. She regarded him anxiously out of
long eyes which mingled grey and green with flecks
of gold, framed in long brown lashes, which matched
her delicate eyebrows above her straight little nose.

'I feel fine,' she answered mechanically, raising herself against her pillows. 'But where am I?'

'The hamlet of Aghios Petros, a mere speck on the
map below Mount Pantokrator,' he told her. 'There's
nothing here except a few fishermen's cottages, so if
you were making for one of the tourist centres I'm
afraid you're wide of the mark.'

'But you're not a fisherman,' she exclaimed, aware
of antagonism in spite of his careless attitude leaning
against the door jamb, his hands thrust into his trouser
pockets, his eyes mere slits as he surveyed her.

'No, and I often wish I were one. Life for them is uncomplicated, simple joys amid a primitive struggle for necessities. We create so many difficulties for ourselves by becoming too civilised and consequently wanting too much.' He straightened himself. 'But I digress. Would you like some coffee?'

'I'd love some, but first, please, how did I come here?'

'I brought you. This is my house.'

'Then it was you who threw the lifebelt?'

'It was, and it was I who pulled you out of the sea. You've been flat out ever since.'

So she owed her life to this arrogant-looking man who seemed to be resenting her presence, for the narrow grey eyes held no friendliness. His reaction to her was disconcerting.

'I was so exhausted,' she excused herself plaintively.

'That was obvious.'

'But I must thank you for rescuing me. I hope it wasn't inconvenient?' She smiled uncertainly but gained no answering smile.

Shrugging his shoulders, he said curtly, 'That was inevitable. I could hardly leave you to drown, and drown you would have done; the currents are swift and uncertain in the strait.'

'Then it was lucky for me that you spotted me. Were you fishing? The boat looked like a caique.'

'It was, and yes, we were ... fishing. The old Corfiote with me thought you were a nereid.' This time he did smile, a puckish grin. 'He wanted me to throw you back into the sea because nereids are supposedly inimical to man.'

'Not always.' She too knew her legends. 'I believe they can even mate happily with humans provided the man never asks where they go when they occasionally disappear.'

'You seem well up in mythology, but if you're human, where did you come from?' He was watching her narrowly. 'Were you washed out to sea by the current? It's a dangerous coast to bathe from if you don't know it, however romantic a midnight swim may be.'

The colour ran up under her thin skin and she plucked nervously at the coverlet. She would have to concoct a story for his benefit, but she had not yet decided what to tell him.

'Yes, I was swept way,' she lied. 'But I had a packet with me, some ... er ... papers.' She looked at him anxiously. 'Did you find it?'

He nodded. 'From which I learned that your name is Rachel Reed.'

'You ... opened it?'

'Naturally. I had to discover you weren't ... a nereid. Do you usually go swimming with your passport and money strapped on your back?'

He had not believed her, and of course he would be a fool if he had.

'Of course not.' She leaned back on her pillows and closed her eyes. 'I ... I don't feel equal to an inquisition just yet.'

She needed time to think, to concoct a convincing story. She had not expected to be confronted by a discerning fellow countryman, though he did not look wholly English in spite of his speech. A few simple peasants could have been fobbed off with a vague yarn, but not him, he was much too sharp.

'I'm sorry,' he said perfunctorily. 'I'll bring you that coffee.'

He went away, leaving the door open, while Rachel

stared after him uneasily. Who was he, and why had he brought her to his house instead of leaving her with the fisherfolk when he obviously resented her? He had looked at her as if she were a slightly revolting speci-men he had under a microscope; and why did he have to wait upon her? Was there no housekeeper, no ser-vant? She looked down at the open collar of the shirt she wore. Who had put her to bed? Not him, surely.

He came back carrying a tray with a mug of coffee, roll and butter on a plate and some fresh peaches. Care-fully he set it across her knees.

'That'll do to be going on with,' he told her. 'We'll have a cooked meal later on. I expect you'll need it after all that exertion. Then I'll run you into Corfu.'

'But ... but I've no clothes.'

'You'll be able to buy some there,' he returned im-perturbably, 'since you're not without funds.'

'I can't go anywhere like this.' She flapped her loose sleeve at him. 'Couldn't your housekeeper or maid lend me something?'

He frowned down at her. 'I live alone.'

'Then ... then last night ...?' she gasped.

A wicked glint came into the narrow pale eyes.

'I couldn't put you to bed in a wet bathing dress.'

Rachel turned hot all over and her cheeks were fiery; she did not know where to look to escape that mocking grey gaze. He laughed at her embarrassment.

'Modesty has to give way to expediency,' he told her. 'You needn't be ashamed of your body, it does credit to the sea nymph idea.'

'Oh, really!' She nearly choked over the coffee which she drank to cover her confusion.

'When you've finished that,' he went on, 'I'd like to know the real reason for your presence in the sea. You were too far out to have been bathing, so don't prevaricate. You must have been dropped overboard from a ship, and since you'd provided yourself with money and papers it must have been deliberate, not an accident or an attempt at suicide, though it might easily have become the latter very successfully.'

She sighed. 'Yes, well, you're entitled to an explanation,' she agreed reluctantly. 'I'll tell you everything when I ... when I've collected myself.'

'You mean when you've cooked up a plausible story,' he commented drily.

She flushed angrily. 'Is there any reason why you should doubt my truthfulness, Mr ... I don't know your name.'

'You've already attempted an evasion,' he pointed out.' My name is Caspar Dakers, and I'm usually known as Cass. My rather dramatic first name was the choice of a Hungarian mother, but I'm a British subject.'

Which accounted for his strange eyes; he was a mingling of two nationalities, and she knew his name.

'I've heard of you,' she told him.

He was famed for brilliant cynical novels as well as his nature writings, and an intriguing personality. Occasionally he did a series on television depicting the flora and fauna of some place he had visited. Rachel had never seen one of them, but she had heard him discussed among her friends.

'I was afraid you might have done,' Cass observed. 'You're not by any chance an importunate fan trying to break into my solitude? I've been plagued by some of those.'

'But of course I am,' she declared brightly, seeing a way out.

He shook his head. 'It won't wash. You'd have known

who I was and where you were if you had been. No,
my dear, you'll have to tell me the true story.'

He went to a cupboard fitted into the wall and opening it extracted a black and gold brocade dressing gown.

'When you get up you can put that on. I expect you'd
rather confront me on your feet.'

'I haven't turned you out of your bedroom?' she
asked in dismay.

'Not entirely. Upon the rare occasions when I've a
visitor, I sleep on a convertible divan in my writing
room or when it's very hot, out of doors. This is a
small house, but elastic.' He went to the door, turning
back to say, 'The bathroom, etc., is next door, there's
hot water and shower.' This time he did shut the
door behind him.

Arrogant and conceited! she thought angrily. She
had heard her mother speak of Cass Dakers, having
met him in the television world, and she had declared
he was attractive. Desirée Lorraine—née Doreen Law-
ton, the first was a pseudonym—was an actress, and
like many of her colleagues frequently changed part-
ners. Cass would not have recognised her married
name of Reed, and in any case her marriage to Angus
Reed had been so brief. Rachel had loved her father
devotedly and was bitterly grieved when her parents
parted. Throughout her childhood years he had been
her sympathiser and her bulwark with and against her
infant woes. But she did not lose him entirely, for although her mother had custody of her and had sent
her to boarding school as soon as she was old enough,
Angus had access to her and she spent most of her
holidays with him until he died prematurely. She loved
her mother too, but with a different sort of feeling, for
Desirée was a little remote, a beautiful goddess on a

pedestal, to be worshipped from afar. She was shocked when she married again, but Angus had told her:

'We can't judge your mother by ordinary standards, she's so lovely and her looks and charm expose her to great temptation. So many men run after her and my successor,' he smiled wryly, 'is a much more exciting fellow than I could ever be.'

Which Rachel hotly denied, Angus was too forgiving.

'You're too young to understand,' he said sadly. 'But don't ever desert her, will you, Ray? The time may come when she needs you badly, and you're her child as well as mine.'

Rachel had been flattered to be told her mother might one day need her, which in her frivolous pursuit of amusement she rarely seemed to do then. She was enthralled by her style and glamour, and swelled with pride when Desirée came to open days at her school, outshining all the other parents. She declared that when Rachel was grown up she would be a companion to her and the girl dreamed of a shared future when they would become close companions. But when she left school she was sadly disillusioned. Although she could not blind herself to Desirée's succession of affairs, she still believed her mother loved her, until ...

Rachel closed her eyes and shivered. She shrank from recalling what had happened, but she was determined Cass Dakers should never discover she was Desirée Lorraine's daughter.

She found the bathroom small but adequate, lined throughout with green tiles. Having showered she put on Cass's shirt again—at least she supposed it was his, as it reached to her knees. She wrapped herself in the equally large robe, turning back the sleeves and looping it up over the girdle. She plaited her hair in two braids, securing the ends with Sellotape which she found in the bathroom cupboard. They hung like a shining rope one over each shoulder, and while she performed her toilet, Rachel decided what she would tell her host.

Leaving the bathroom, she pattered across the hall in search of him, anxious to tell her story and test his reaction. The house was actually a bungalow and all the rooms opened on to a square hall in its centre lit by a skylight. Her room was at the side, but the living room in front faced the sea. Through its open door she glimpsed french windows opening on to a terrace and was unable to resist an impulse to go outside. As she passed through the room she noticed it contained some comfortable-looking chairs, bright rugs on the floor and a few pictures on the walls, which made it appear less bare than her bedroom. Stepping through the window, she was faced with a glorious view of the sea, the house being built on a cliff looking down upon the roofs of the fishing hamlet some way below. The land on either side enclosed the cove like a pair of tree-clad arms, thrusting out into the blue-green sea and terminating in ridges of bone-white rocks. In the distance loomed the misty mountains of Albania. On the other three sides the house was surrounded by trees, oaks, pines and olives climbing the hillside and forming dense cover to enclose it. The place was enclosed in a green bower, except for the frontage looking out to sea. Over the balustrade that separated the terrace from the cliff top was a tangle of climbing roses.

Rachel drew breaths of the warm scented air and felt her courage and spirits revive. The bungalow was an ideal hideout, if only she could persuade Cass to allow her to stay hidden there for a few days. Nobody would discover her in such an isolated spot; it was as impregnable as an eagle's eyrie, with only a winding track through the trees connecting it with the village. Unfortunately he seemed to resent her presence, so it would not be easy, and she determined to use every artifice she could command to gain her end. If rumour did not lie Cass Dakers was susceptible to a pretty face, and without being unduly vain she knew she had her share of good looks. He had already rescued her once, and given up his room to her need, sooner than leave her to fend for herself among the villagers. He could not be devoid of chivalrous impulses and it was up to her to appeal to him to continue with his kindness to the extent of giving her refuge for a little longer.

CHAPTER TWO

RACHEL'S reverie was rudely broken by a hand gripping her shoulder and whirling her round to thrust her back into the room behind her. Cass had come upon her with noiseless tread and had whisked her inside without ceremony.

'Are you crazy?' he demanded. 'Do you want everybody to know you're here?'

'It's so lovely outside and there's no one about,' she protested. She, more than he, did not want to advertise her presence, but there was no one in sight.

'*You* didn't see anyone but boys climb up into the woods, and they've got eyes like a hawk for strangers.'

Rachel rubbed her shoulder which she was sure his grip had bruised and looked at him speculatively. She had a good reason for wishing to hide herself which she had not yet divulged, but there seemed no need for him to be so rough.

'Have you got a girl-friend who would object to my presence?' she hazarded, for that seemed a possible explanation for his violent action.

'My girl-friends are as numerous as Solomon's wives,' he returned flippantly, 'but I don't bring them here. This is my retreat when I've had enough of carousing in London. There's a great charm in contrasts. There I live a convivial existence, here I enjoy solitude but I have to fight to preserve it, and if it gets around that I've got a woman here there'll be nasty little paragraphs in the popular press about famous author's Corfiote love nest. They call it the human touch, I term it damned impertinence.'

'I agree with you,' she said, thinking his almost Spartan furnishings did not suggest anything so glamorous as an illicit romance. 'But that being so, I'm surprised you brought me here. Isn't there a taverna where you could have dumped me?'

Though his bungalow was ideally situated for her purpose, she did not like being considered an imposition.

'Aghios Petros has no such amenities,' he informed her. 'The fishermen's dwellings are very primitive with no accommodation for visitors, so I had no alternative. After all, you're a compatriot, and I don't suppose you speak Greek.'

'I'm afraid you're right,' she said ruefully, 'but since I am here, couldn't you put up with me for a few days?' She looked at him eagerly. 'I promise I'll keep out of your way and I won't go outside, and I ... well, the truth is I want to disappear for a while.'

He refused to meet her pleading eyes.

'You nearly disappeared for good,' he reminded her gruffly.

She sighed deeply. 'That would have solved all my problems, · wouldn't it?' she observed pathetically, hoping to arouse his sympathy, but he appeared to be blandly indifferent.

'You haven't told me what they are,' he pointed out. 'So far we've established that you jumped off a passing boat but not the why and wherefore. Don't tell me you did it to escape a fate worse than death. That's too corny.'

There was derision in the narrow grey eyes and mockery in his deep voice, which raised her ire. With difficulty controlling her temper, she informed him :

'For once your corny phrase was accurate.'

'Never!' he laughed scornfully. 'You mean you couldn't cope? That isn't my experience of modern girls.'

'I couldn't cope with Panos Simonides.'

He started at the mention of that name. Simonides, the millionaire Greek ship-owner, and his luxurious yacht the *Nausicaa* frequently visited Corfu, where he was well known. The man was a notorious libertine.

'Death would be preferable to him,' Rachel said simply.

'Not every woman would agree with you.' Cass' tone was very dry. 'I believe he pays lavishly for favours received. But do you mean to tell me *you* were on board the *Nausicaa*?' She did not look in the least like the smart sophisticated women Panos usually had in tow. 'How come?'

'Because I was an unsuspecting idiot,' Rachel declared passionately, and that was nearly the truth. 'I was misled ...'

'Really?' he cut in contemptuously. 'Are you sure you weren't doing a little amateur gold-digging and panicked when you were presented with the bill?'

Rachel stared at his smooth brown face without at first understanding his meaning and then when it reached her, her face flamed. She did not stop to think that anyone who had met Panos Simonides, and Cass probably had, could believe any girl would be so naïve as not to realise what he was, and he must be thinking she was either an idiot or a wanton. Indignation swamped her need to placate him and she flashed angrily :

'How dare you suggest such a thing? I'm not that sort of girl.'

'Forgive me,' he returned without any penitence in face or voice, 'but I'm hardly in a position to judge what you are upon so short an acquaintanceship, am I?'

She recognised that was reasonable, and Caspar Dakers, being a wordly cynic, would think the worse of everybody. She cast about in her mind for a means to convince him of her integrity, but none presented itself. To have been in Simonides' company was no recommendation for a virtuous girl, as he knew only too well, and she could not divulge the real reason for her presence on the yacht. So she said nothing, but stood shamefaced with drooping head which seemed weighed down by her long plaits. Cass glanced at her and away again, biting his lips. Rachel had no inkling, how could she have, that it would be painful to him to be confronted daily by that gleaming hair and pale oval face which stirred bitter memories. She only sensed that he was antagonistic to her for some unknown reason, which made her task of appealing to his pity all the more difficult.

'Sit down, girl,' he commanded brusquely. 'And get on with your story. How were you misled?'

He waited for her to seat herself in one of the two armchairs, then taking a hard upright one, he turned it about and sat astride it, his arms folded along its back, looking at her enquiringly. Rachel appeared small and slight in the big chair, her enveloping robe wrapped closely around her. Her ordeal had left her pale and shadow-eyed even after her long sleep. She looked very young, vulnerable and innocent, but the man regarding her knew by bitter experience how deceptive such an appearance could be. Unconsciously he had assumed the attitude of a counsel for the prosecution, his steely eyes fixed sternly upon her downcast face. As she seemed at a loss how to begin, he recapitulated.

'Your name is Rachel Reed, you're of British birth, and you're twenty years old—I gleaned that from your passport. Go on from there.'

'May I remind you, you haven't returned it?'

'All in good time. I suppose it *is* your passport?'

'What a nasty suspicious mind you have!' she exclaimed. 'Of course it's mine.'

'No of course about it, you're shrouded in mystery. Proceed.'

He's horrible, she thought, and only prudence restrained her from telling him so. She twisted her hands together nervously while she embarked upon the story she had invented for his benefit.

'I answered an advertisement for a secretary, that's my sort of job, you know.' (It was not, but she trusted he would never discover that misrepresentation) 'I . . . I thought a sea trip would be fun. It was all right to begin with, I'd no suspicion Mr Simonides was . . . was like he is. It wasn't until we were approaching Corfu, he . . . he made a pass at me, and told me my duties . . . weren't quite what I'd expected. I knew nobody on the ship would dare to help me, so I . . . tried to escape.'

Becoming colour had run up under her thin skin during her recital, but now it retreated leaving her paler than before.

'In fact you were incredibly naïve and stupid,' Cass told her bluntly.

She looked down at her bare toes, curling and uncurling on the mat upon which they rested.

'I ... I suppose I was.'

'Like all your generation you rushed bullheaded into an escapade with which you were unable to cope,' he said severely, 'and expect other people to get you out of your difficulties.'

'Are you then so ancient?' she countered, feeling she hated him. 'Don't you ever make mistakes?'

'Of course, but I'm old enough to have learned some caution, and your so-called fun is another name for licence,' he said repressively.

Rachel turned her head away from that accusing stare. She wanted to tell him to go to hell, and if rumour did not lie, he was in no position to censure other people's conduct, but she restrained herself, because his place was the sort of refuge she needed and she did not want to be summarily evicted. Cass saw the rebellious flash in her eyes and smiled sourly. Yanni was right, this girl was born to create trouble.

'Haven't you got any parents?' he went on, as she did not speak. 'Wouldn't they help you? Last night you spoke of your father.'

'He's dead,' she said flatly, concealing the ache in her heart. If Angus were still alive she would not be in her present situation. She threw Cass an anxious glance wondering what else she had said in her semi-conscious state; nothing very revealing presumably or there would be no need for this inquisition.

Cass was noticing the delicate lines of her neck and chin; the disturbing likeness was still there, but it could only be coincidence. As he had told Dion, there were plenty of girls with ash-blonde hair.

'And your mother?' he snapped, determined not to weaken.

'We're ... estranged.'

'Poor little orphan Annie!' Cass exclaimed, and laughed.

Rachel clenched her hands.

'It's not funny,' she rebuked him. 'I'm alone in the world ... now.'

'I'm sorry,' he said perfunctorily. 'When you jumped into the sea, did you imagine you could reach Corfu?'

'It didn't look very far from the yacht and I'm a good swimmer.'

'But your chances were nil against the currents, and if you had landed what did you intend to do then?'

'I thought I could hide in some village until Mr Simonides had gone on to Athens where he was bound.'

'A perfectly crazy notion. They'd have reported you or thrown you back into the sea as an undesirable presence.' He was remembering Yanni's reaction.

She shook her head in disbelief.

'I'm sure they wouldn't. I've always understood the Greeks were overwhelmingly hospitable. But you were wonderful.' She clasped her hands, raising wide beseeching eyes to his. 'It was you who saved my life and I'm sure you won't abandon me now.'

'I've every intention of doing just that,' he told her grimly. 'I'm going to take you to the Consulate in Corfu before the day is out. They're the proper people to deal with you.'

'No!' she cried vehemently, and her glance went round the room like that of a hunted hare. She dared not appear in Corfu until she was sure the *Nausicaa* had left. 'Please ... please, no. Simonides will be looking for me there.'

'What if he is? You're a British subject, the Consulate will protect you.'

'I ... I don't know. He ... he has a lot of influence.'
She was stammering in her fear. It was not only
Simonides who would be there, and how could she
explain her predicament to the authorities, when it
was not quite what she had represented to her host?
'Oh, don't let him get me,' she begged.

'He certainly seems to have put the wind up you,'
Cass remarked drily. 'Do you imagine he might kidnap
you?'

'It's possible.'

Cass frowned. He knew it was, though he would
hardly credit that the Greek would take so much trouble
to recover a silly girl.

'Then what alternative do you suggest?'

Rachel looked round the pleasant sunlit room which
seemed such a harbour of refuge.

'It's so isolated here,' she began diffidently. 'If only
you'd let me stay for a few days until they've stopped
looking for me ...' He gave an impatient exclamation
and her heart sank. 'Then perhaps I could hide somewhere along the coast, a cave—there must be some. If
you'd just give me a little food ...' Her big eyes be-
sought him frantically.

'Don't be absurd,' he said roughly.

Rachel realised that she would never prevail with
him by reasoning, she would have to do something
more dramatic.

'Sooner than go to Corfu, I'll go back into the sea,'
she declared.

Cass rose to his feet and began to pace the room,
his winged eyebrows knotted in thought. There was
something here that baffled him, for her story did not
call for such desperation. A rash girl had taken a
situation without proper safeguards and her employer

had made a pass at her. To avoid his attentions she had jumped into the sea, but had had the forethought to arm herself with her money and passport. Simonides, being a man of the world, would only shrug his shoulders and dismiss her as a little nitwit. He would have to report her loss at Athens or Corfu, but it was unlikely he would pursue her further, so that her panic seemed unreasonable, unless she was putting on an act for his benefit. Some of this he tried to convey to her, but Rachel would not accept his arguments, she insisted that she would drown herself or take a chance on the mountainside sooner than risk encountering Simonides again. Cass sighed with exasperation.

'To harbour you here would be illegal,' he told her.

'Not as a visitor,' she returned promptly. 'I don't have to report for at least a week, and I'm willing to pay for my keep.'

'The devil you are! Don't you understand, I don't want you here. I've some ... er ... acquaintances on the island, Greeks of good family who respect the conventions if you don't. What will they think if they discover I'm alone with a strange girl?'

'They needn't see me,' she pointed out. 'I'll hide if anyone comes.' She paused, then added beguilingly, 'I could do the chores while you get on with your writing.'

'Which is what I should be doing now—what's more, I'm behind with my schedule which you're interrupting.'

'Then you mustn't waste any more time taking me into Corfu,' she declared triumphantly. 'I could get the meals for you while you're working.'

Cass ran his fingers through his thick hair. She could not know how her presence distracted him and he was anxious to be rid of her.

'Persistent, aren't you?' he growled.

'No, desperate,' she corrected him. She stood up, a forlorn figure in the borrowed robe, and searched his face for a sign of relenting. There was none, and with a deep sigh she moved across the room.

'Since you won't help me, I'll go.'

'Where?'

'Does it matter to you? The woods ... the sea ... I'd sooner drown than go to Corfu!'

She walked past him towards the door. She had no plan, she only knew she must leave this house unless Cass had a change of heart, which from his grim expression and rigid form was unlikely. He had not even remembered that he held her money and passport, but she would not deign to ask for them. Childishly she thought that if she starved or drowned he might be sorry he had let her go, which gave her a dreary kind of satisfaction.

Rachel opened the door, striving to preserve a dignified calm. She had in fact crossed its threshold when he hurried after her, his hand closing urgently upon her arm, and pulled her back into the room.

'Damn it all, girl, I'm not a brute,' he exploded. 'I can't let you go wandering about the island in my dressing-gown without even shoes on your feet. I'll see if I can find a pair of espadrilles ...'

'It doesn't matter,' she interrupted tonelessly. 'I shan't need footwear in the sea, into which you're driving me.'

He was standing so close to her she caught a whiff of aftershave and eau-de-cologne from his morning ablutions. The hand gripping her arm was long-fingered and well shaped. The realisation of his masculinity caused her to shiver. She was raw from recent experiences and shrank from the maleness of him. Cass sensed her recoil with a touch of pique. Women did not usually shrink from him, but his feelings were far from amorous, as apparently were hers, which robbed the situation of any spice.

Standing with his back against the door, he told her:

'You can get this straight before we go any further. I've got a girl, and she mustn't know of your presence here. She'd resent it bitterly.'

So that was what he meant by conventional Greek acquaintances.

'I'd hate to disrupt your romance,' she returned with a gleam of spirit. 'I suppose I ought to be grateful to you for saving my life,' she continued despondently. 'But oh, God, I wish you hadn't.'

A wave of desolation swept over her with the realisation of her friendless state. She stumbled back towards her chair and collapsed into it, and because she was still weak from her ordeal, tears rose to her eyes and spilled down her cheeks. She wept soundlessly and hopelessly, putting her hands before her face, for she did not possess a handkerchief to wipe her eyes.

Cass moved uncomfortably. 'Stop it, girl,' he demanded.

Then he was sitting on the arm of her chair, his arm round her shoulders and his own clean white handkerchief was thrust between her fingers.

'Crying won't help,' he said gently, but it had, for he was softening towards her. She appeared so frail and helpless, the bones of her shoulders were slight and fragile to his touch. Cass was tender towards all weak, defenceless creatures and she was like a stray kitten or puppy seeking shelter whom he had rebuffed.

Rachel wiped her eyes. Her tears had been perfectly genuine, and she had not expected he would be affected by them; that he had was encouraging. She made a definite movement of withdrawal from his encircling arm and instantly he removed it, but he remained perched on the arm of the chair and something in his expression made her faintly uneasy. She was beginning to recall some of the gossip she had heard about Caspar Dakers, and having just extricated herself from one dangerous situation it would be folly to plunge into another. Cass, when he was not vegetating in his Corfiote retreat, lived it up in London and Paris. Possessing private means as well as his considerable earnings he could splash money around and did. He was also notorious for his affairs, but of late he had spent more time in Corfu and less in the public eye. The attraction must be the Greek girl he had mentioned and that had been a warning to keep off the grass. Rachel decided she had nothing to fear from him and a great deal to gain if she could persuade him to conceal her until Simonides had vanished over the horizon. A moment ago that had seemed impossible, but his changed attitude raised her hopes.

She laid a confiding hand upon his knee and looked up at him with tear-stained eyes, smiling wanly.

'I'm so sorry, I didn't mean to ... er ... blackmail you again. Perhaps one of the fishermen would take me in? The one who was with you on the caique?'

'That he wouldn't.' Cass laughed recalling Yanni's insistence that the girl was not human and would bring bad luck. 'Don't talk rubbish,' he went on roughly, unwillingly yielding to the appeal in her strangely coloured eyes. At least they were different and recalled no hurtful memories. 'You can stay here for the present until we discover if Simonides has left the vicinity.'

He looked down at her hand upon his knee. It was not a specially small hand, in fact it looked capable, but it was delicately formed, with slim white fingers, and almond-shaped nails that had been well tended. Hands are as individual as faces and though her eyes were unfamiliar, her hand was not. Cass regarded it as if it were a noxious insect, then very deliberately placed it on her lap.

Rachel had drawn a long breath of relief; she had won after all, but it had been a hard battle. She regarded his rejection of her hand as a reminder that he was not a free man, and murmured :

'I'll be for ever in your debt, but I'd hate to come between you and your girl. Warn me when you're expecting her and I'll hide.'

He gave her an odd look, seemed about to say something and checked himself.

'You said she was Greek,' Rachel went on, becoming curious. 'I suppose she's very beautiful. Many Greek girls are.'

A mischievous glint came into his slanted eyes.

'A real Aphrodite,' he told her. 'Perfect figure, regular features, dark hair and burning eyes. You know the type?'

Rachel nodded. 'If I see anyone answering to that description appearing I'll bolt for cover.' Having gained his leave to stay she was anxious to be co-operative.

'You needn't worry, she never comes here.'

Rachel opened her eyes very wide. 'Oh? Why?'

He got to his feet without answering and moved away as if he found her questions irritating.

'Simonides may be detained in Corfu to attend the inquest.'

She wrinkled her delicate eyebrows. 'Inquest? What inquest?'

'On you, of course. You'll have to be presumed drowned.'

This seemed to her to be slightly macabre, when she was sitting there very much alive, almost as though she were a ghost.

'Perhaps he won't report that I'm missing.'

Cass swung round. 'He couldn't be such a swine. Of course he'll make enquiries.'

'He's every sort of swine,' Rachel assured him. She began to play with one of her plaits. 'I shouldn't think he'll make any public enquiries, they might embarrass him.'

'But you can't just disappear. Surely someone will want to know what's become of you?'

Rachel sighed. Once she would have answered that there was very definitely someone who would care deeply, but she had only been a pawn in that person's squalid game, and since she had been a disappointment she would not be regretted.

'I told you I'd no family,' she said quietly. 'When I'm sure the coast is clear I'll go back to England and get a job.'

Cass regarded her critically. In spite of her peculiar garb she looked too dainty, too unsophisticated to be capable of fending for herself. She was the type of girl who needed protecting, as her story showed, who appealed to a man's chivalrous instincts; she had even got round him by using her femininity.

'You don't look like a working girl,' he said bluntly.

'I possess certain skills,' she returned. 'For instance, I'm quite a good cook.' It was the one really useful thing she had learned at her expensive school. 'I can at least prepare your meals for you while I'm here.'

He grinned suddenly. 'I'm not partial to elegant little messes, I like man-sized food.'

'I'm sure you do. Good plain fare, I can manage that.' He had told her he did not employ domestic help, and she enquired:

'Do you cater for yourself?'

'And cook except when I go out, which isn't often.'

'Versatile man—author, playwright, television personality, fisherman and cook!'

The slanted eyebrows drew together as he regarded her dubiously.

'You seem to be well informed about my activities.'

'You're well known. I told you I'd heard of you.'

'Have you read any of my books?' he asked, prompted by the egoism of the author.

'My father was a great admirer of your work.' She paused, biting her lip; it was still painful to recall memories of her father. 'I've only read one myself, it was very clever. *Serpents in Paradise*, it was called, but ... but ...' She had not liked it at all and only read it at Angus' insistence. It had been too horribly cynical.

'That one was not a book for children,' he told her loftily.

'I'm not a child, I'm twenty,' she protested.

'A vast age,' he mocked. 'You should have tried one of the nature books, they're quite innocuous.'

She did not tell him she preferred romantic novels, he would only despise her taste. He must be very, very clever and sophisticated to write such books. She had not fully understood the one she had read, and its descriptions of human depravity had shocked her. Cass was miles above her in experience and erudition. Even her mother, so critical of men, had quoted his legendary exploits with admiration—daredevil actions as if he wanted to prove he was not an emasculated writer, but which unkind critics said were self-advertisement. His girl-friend must be a very superior person to herself to have won his regard. Of anyone else she would have said love, but Caspar Dakers, according to his books, was far too cynical a person to do anything so human as to fall in love.

Cass was watching the expressions flit across her mobile face as she made her assessment with amusement. He knew the sort of gossip she would have heard about him.

'Perhaps now you've remembered my reputation you'd feel safer among the fishermen,' he suggested with a derisive glint in his narrow grey eyes.

'Oh, I wouldn't be in any danger from you, I'm far too insignificant,' she returned promptly, 'and I'm sure you wouldn't be scared of flouting conventions.'

His slanted black brows rose comically.

'Do you consider I'm so immoral?'

'I didn't meant that, but I've always heard that you feared neither God nor man.'

'Ssh!' He glanced round the room with pretended anxiety. 'Haven't you heard that Corfu is the Garden of the Gods? They must be respected in their own purlieus.'

'Surely you can't be superstitious? I've also been told that it might be the place described in Shakespeare's *The Tempest*.'

'And also the scene of Odysseus' little affair with Nausicaa. Undoubtedly a land of magic.' He dropped his frivolous tone and became serious. 'It was until the tourist racket began and it was desecrated with bigger and bigger hotels. But there are still places that the blight hasn't reached. Here, for example.'

'But don't you think it's only right that the beauties of nature should be available to everyone?' she asked earnestly.

'The majority don't come for the beauties of nature,' he returned. 'They come for the sunshine and the amenities of the hotels, bringing their noise and pollution with them. But let's get down to practical matters. I'll have to go somewhere and get you some clothes.'

'I hate to have to bother you, but I'd feel less conspicuous in jeans and a shirt,' she agreed. 'This garment ...' she waggled the embroidered sleeve of his robe, 'is very decorative, but impractical. And I can't go out in my swimsuit.'

'Which wouldn't be at all conspicuous in Corfu,' he remarked coolly, 'but since you'd sooner die than go there, I'll do what I can.' He took a piece of paper and a pen out of a drawer. 'What are your measurements?'

Rachel gave him her vital statistics with slightly heightened colour. She wanted to hold aloof from him, since his hospitality had been offered so reluctantly, and make herself as unobtrusive as possible, but necessity was forcing her into intimacy.

'Just a shirt, trousers and a pair of shoes,' she suggested. 'And ... and something to sleep in.'

'And underwear.'

'I couldn't expect you to get that,' she said hastily.

Cass grinned impishly.

'You'll need a change,' he remarked imperturbably. 'I know what girls wear, I'd be blind if I didn't, and I've got your bust size.' Rachel blushed and his grin broadened. 'Television advertisements make sure men know all about feminine fripperies,' he went on. His narrowed eyes were mere slits between his thick lashes and brimming with mischief. 'And I haven't reached mature years without some personal experience.'

'Indeed?' Rachel became very cool. The last thing she wanted was for Cass to become fresh, for she was entirely in his power, and his obvious enjoyment of her bashfulness was ominous. But she did not think he was the sort of man to take advantage of her helplessness, in spite of his reputation. She had nothing to go upon except instinct and that might prove wrong, but it was reassuring that he had been careful to tell her he was involved with a Greek beauty.

Noticing the faint anxiety in her eyes, he laughed.

'I've written television scripts and helped produce them. The studios don't leave much to the imagination; nor am I interested in seducing innocents.'

That information needled her.

'I'm not all that innocent,' she declared sharply. 'A girl has to know her way about these days.'

'Yours led you on to Simonides' yacht,' he reminded her. 'And if you hadn't been an innocent you'd be there still.'

That silenced her, and at the mention of the Greek magnate's name, the hunted look came back into her eyes.

'You won't tell anyone I'm here?'

'That's the last thing I want to advertise,' he declared fervently. 'Well, I'd better get on with the shopping.'

Rachel jumped up hastily. 'You'll use my money, of course. Incidentally, you haven't returned it yet.'

He regarded her quizzically. 'It's in travellers'

cheques which you have to change in person. For the present you'll have to be in my debt.'

'Which I am already, more than I can say . . .'

He held up his hand to check her.

'No sob-stuff, please, we've had enough of that.'

She winced, for she had wept in his presence and she did not cry easily. Like most men he shrank from women's tears.

'We'll have a reckoning up when the time comes,' he went on. 'For the present your money and passport are safer in my safe. Oh yes,' as she looked surprised, 'I have a small safe, though it's not really necessary. Nobody here would touch anyone else's property. Incidentally, since you say you can cook, you might rustle up some lunch while I'm away. You'll find the larder is well stocked.'

He was gone, striding out into the sunlit exterior, leaving Rachel with mixed feelings. She was grateful to him for giving her asylum, but his derisory manner and the mocking glint in his eyes discomposed her. She did not know whether he believed her tale or not, or how far she could trust him, but there was nowhere else where she could go.

She heard the car start up and the sound of its engine fading away as it nosed its way down the rough track through the trees. Once she was properly clad she would feel more confident to deal with Cass and any other problems that might arise. Meanwhile she felt she had been challenged to produce an appetising meal and that she would endeavour to do. She went in search of the kitchen hoping it was not as primitive as she feared it might be.

CHAPTER THREE

To Rachel's surprised delight the kitchen was fitted with modern equipment. The floor was red-tiled, the large window looked out into the surrounding trees divided from them by an open space filled with flowering shrubs, the scent of which filled the room. It was at the back of the house and the wooded slopes ascended far above her line of sight, obliterating the sky. There was an electric cooker, whether the supply was main or provided by its own generator she did not know, and either would be very expensive, but then Cass had plenty of money and he had not stinted it upon his kitchen though the rest of the house was a little austere. There were two large refrigerators, one a deep-freeze, several cupboards painted white, a formica-topped table, stainless steel sink, washing machine and draining board all conveniently arranged in one unit. Investigation of the well stocked cupboard suggested that Cass liked Italian food, and Rachel decided she would make Spaghetti Bolognaise.

The tray of breakfast things stood on the drainer, and she started operations by washing up. The brocade robe proved an impediment with its flapping sleeves which refused to stay rolled up and the shirt was nearly as tiresome. Finding her swimsuit hung over the back of a chair, she abandoned her borrowed drapery and clad only in the bathing dress, which was in one piece, she felt more comfortable. She discovered hanging on a rail along with the tea towels a plastic apron, one of the

43

sort advertising drinks that have become so popular.
This one had Cinzano written across the chest and was
in red, white and blue. Rachel put it on, wondering
what Cass looked like in it, and giggled at the picture it
evoked. She was rummaging in a drawer looking for
kitchen spoons when a voice behind her caused her to
start like a nervous horse.

'Kalimera.'

She spun round and saw standing in the doorway a
slim dark youth of about eighteen or nineteen, she
judged; his still boyish limbs were tanned to a rich dark
brown, his face had the regular features common among
Greeks, with a pair of magnificent dark eyes, the lashes
sticking out like spiders' legs, and a full-lipped well
shaped mouth. His scalp was covered by a mass of black
curls which clung to his head and he had not permitted
to grow long. He was the handsomest youth she had
ever seen, but she had been foolish not to lock the back
door after Cass's departure. But with open windows
everywhere it was not going to be easy to conceal her
presence, unless she kept the curtains drawn which
had not occurred to her. She had not expected anybody
to come prowling round.

The lad was smiling, displaying even white teeth,
and he held in one hand a string of fish which he had
apparently just caught. His gaze was fixed upon her
with the directness common among his countrymen and
from his expression he appreciated what he saw. Rachel
wished she was not so scantily clad, but reflected that
he must be used to seeing foreign girls in bathing gear
along the coast.

She stared at him a little helplessly, wondering what
to do. He had walked in as if he were familiar with the
place without knocking and so giving her a chance to

hide. Cass would be annoyed, but he had not warned her she might have a visitor, and if she was going to prepare a meal, she had to be in the kitchen.

The youth did not seem surprised to see her and he made some remark in which she caught the word *thalassa*. That she did know meant sea, and it flashed into her mind that he might have been one of the crew of the caique that had rescued her, in which case he would know where Cass had taken her. So she nodded and smiled, waiting for his next move.

'Kyrios Dakers?'

She hardly recognised his pronunciation of the name, he was evidently expecting to see Cass. She shook her head and pointed out of the window.

'Corfu.'

He crossed the kitchen with a lithe catlike movement and laid his offering on the sink. Then he indicated the cooker, saying something which she could not understand, but plainly indicating that she should deal with them. The fish, some Mediterranean variety that was unfamiliar to her, looked beautifully fresh and would no doubt make a tasty meal, but though she had been ready to deal with spaghetti, she baulked at cleaning fish. That, in the elegant establishment where she had gone to be 'finished' after leaving school, was not included in the curriculum for Cordon Bleu cookery that she had taken. She regarded them doubtfully, while the youth seemed to be cudgelling his brains for the few English words he had picked up from Cass and other visitors. Finally he came out with:

'Dinner, cook—not keep.'

Rachel picked up a fish and looked at it helplessly. As if sensing her distaste, he took it from her and with the assurance of long habit took a knife from a drawer

and began to deal with it. Relieved by his co-operation,
Rachel fetched a dish and he laid the neatly filleted
sections upon it. Then he cleaned up the rather revolting debris, wrapped it in paper and put it into the gar-
bage pail. He seemed to know where everything was
and she concluded that he often came to help Cass
about the house. If anyone were to blame for his intrusion it was the master, who had not thought to mention he might appear.

It was too soon to grill the fish as Cass could not be
back for some time, so she put the dish in the fridge
and feeling that her visitor deserved some reward, suggested:

'Coffee?'

That he understood, but he shook his head. Instead
he went to the fridge and took out orange juice and ice.
Deftly he filled two glasses and offered one to her, with
a bow.

Rachel accepted it and sat down on one of the high
stools of which there were several round the table and
indicated with a gesture that he should do likewise.
Smiling, he obeyed, then pointing to himself he said:

'Dion.'

Copying his gesture, she said in her turn:

'Rachel.'

He beamed delightedly, then began a complicated
pantomime which confirmed her supposition that he
had been one of her rescuers. He was very friendly and
frankly curious, contradicting Cass's assertion that the
natives would be suspicious and hostile. She was guiltily
aware that her host would not approve of this fraternis-
ing with the populace, but did not see that she could do
anything about it. Dion had not been surprised to find
her there and she could not snub someone who had

helped to pull her out of the sea, and since he was there she might as well enjoy his company, though communication was restricted since neither knew the other's language, but his eloquent eyes showed plainly that he admired her.

Realising that time was passing, Rachel stood up, carried her glass to the sink and started her preparations. To follow the fish she had planned to make a cheese soufflé. Dion now proved invaluable, anticipating whatever she needed before she could look for it with almost uncanny foresight. His domestic knowledge was surprising, since the male Greek does not deign to assist his womenfolk in what he considers is their domain. Cass must have trained him to do a share of his bachelor chores. It is always difficult working in a strange place without knowing where anything is, and she was grateful for his help.

With the fish under the grill, the soufflé in the oven, Dion assisted her to lay the table. He indicated that Cass ate in the kitchen, forestalling her movement towards the living room by barring her way and shaking his head. He produced a red check tablecloth and showed her where the cutlery was, himself setting it out. Then she was in a dilemma, wondering if she ought to ask him to join them, but it was hardly her place to do so, and he did not seem to expect an invitation as he laid only two places.

Returning from his errand, Cass found the pair of them, his guest lightly clad in a swimsuit and plastic apron, laughing with Dion about some slight mishap over the sink.

'*Kalimera, kyrie!*'

Dion turned to greet him with a wide welcoming smile, but Rachel, seeing the ominous scowl upon his face, wilted, waiting for the storm to break. Cass was holding a carrier bag filled with parcels and he thrust it towards her.

'Go and make yourself decent,' he snapped.

Rachel had forgotten her scanty apparel. In spite of his admiring glances, Dion had not made her feel self-conscious. Now she became painfully aware of her appearance. Snatching the bag from Cass, she fled into her bedroom.

She dressed quickly in brassiere, panties, green drip-dry trousers and green tee-shirt, a colour that brought out the green in her hazel eyes. The garments were not quite what she had asked for, but Cass certainly knew what would suit her. The underwear caused her a qualm. Had he selected it or asked the assistant to do so? She hoped the latter. There was something about Cass that made such familiarity distasteful to her. It was his virile masculinity that struck some responsive chord in her own being. Without altogether understanding, her instinct scented danger. Give him an inch and he'd take a mile, she thought gloomily.

She returned to dish up the meal and found Dion had been asked to stay, for he had laid another place. He would have explained his presence by the gift of the fish, and it was delicious. The soufflé was done to a turn, and they finished with fresh fruit which Cass had brought with him. Throughout the meal he conversed with Dion, occasionally translating a phrase for Rachel's benefit. The boy was anxious to know if she had fully recovered from her ordeal, but with innate good manners refrained from asking how long she would be staying, but his fine eyes resting now upon her, and then his host, were questioning. He was evidently intrigued by the situation. Then he said something that brought

from Cass a vehement denial and he looked puzzled. As
for Cass, he seemed to be restraining himself with difficulty and Rachel sensed he was angry with her,
though she could not think where she had erred. She
could not help Dion's intrusion, surely he must realise
that? And from their easy intimacy it was obvious he
had frequent contact with the Greek youth. The food
had been prepared to perfection, he could not fault
that, so why his wrath?

She made coffee, and when they had drunk it, Dion
rose to his feet, evidently declaring he must go. Cass
slapped him on the shoulder and thanked him for the
fish. Rachel held out her hand and he raised it on the
back of his to touch his brow, a curious gesture expressing homage. Then he gave her a wide smile and said:

'You most lovely,' and glanced at Cass to see if he
had used the right words.

'Get along with you, you flatterer,' Cass bade him in
English. 'Where did you learn to say that?'

Dion smiled again beatifically, bowed to them both
and went out, springing down the hillside like a young
gazelle.

Rachel started to clear the table.

'Leave that,' Cass said sharply. 'You can do it later
when I've had my say.' He looked her up and down
with insolent appraisal. 'Yanni had the right idea,' he
went on harshly. 'I should have thrown you back into
the sea. Women like you are a menace, but understand
once and for all, I will not have you seducing the
native youths.'

Rachel stared at him aghast. His eyes were mere slits
of venom, his tone inimical. How could he so mis-
construe a pleasant innocent interlude?

'I'd no intention of doing any such thing,' she de-

clared indignantly. 'He came in before I realised he
was there, so I'd no chance to hide, and I gather he has
the run of the place. Anyway, he couldn't understand
a word I said.'

'He didn't need to,' Cass sneered. 'There you were,
three-quarters naked, flaunting yourself like the tart
you probably are, every line of you provocative invitation.' Rachel's eyes flashed. 'Dion's a simple lad with an
impeccable girl-friend lined up for him with parental
approval. I will not have you throwing a spanner in
the works.'

'You're being absurd,' she retorted, trembling with
anger. 'I couldn't work in those trailing garments and
it's warm in here. Don't tell me Dion hasn't seen dozens
of girls in bikinis, and I did have on a regulation swimsuit plus your apron. Corfu isn't all that archaic.'

'Dion rarely goes to Corfu, he spends his time in the
village, where the old ways persist. Unmarried girls
aren't permitted to talk to young men alone. It's unfortunate that Dion chose this morning to bring me a
present, but there was no need to be intimate with him.'

'I was only being friendly,' she said defensively, then
with a flash of spirit, 'I wouldn't have expected the
author of *Serpents in Paradise* to be so prudish! That
was outspoken to an almost unpleasant degree.'

'So you found my book unpleasant?' Cass looked
dangerous. 'It was at least honest, I don't deal in
euphemisms. But we weren't talking about me, we were
discussing Dion.'

Rachel dimpled provocatively, and her big eyes
sparkled. She thought Cass was making a ridiculous
fuss about nothing and could not imagine what was
annoying him, though there did seem to be some subtle
undercurrent which she was unable to understand.

'Dion is a very charming boy,' she declared.

Cass groaned. 'Rachel Reed, will you please leave him alone? If you hurt him I'll never forgive myself for allowing you to stay here.'

Rachel stared at him disdainfully.

'Mr Dakers, what precisely do you think I am?'

'A girl, of course, with all the predatory instincts of the modern uninhibited miss. It's common knowledge that foreign girls holidaying abroad are on the outlook for a bit of fun, as they call it, with the local lads. Most of the boys can give as good as they get, but Dion is unsophisticated. He's my protégé and I feel responsible for him.'

'But we weren't doing anything,' Rachel protested. 'I'd never willingly harm him. He was like a young brother ...'

Cass interrupted her by bursting out laughing and she looked at him reproachfully.

'I doubt if Dion's reactions were fraternal,' he said when his amusement had subsided. 'You see, your arrival was romantically dramatic, which would appeal to him, and unfortunately you're very beautiful.'

'Wh-at?' she stammered. It was the last thing she had expected him to say. She did not feel beautiful, she had not even been able to brush her hair, he had seen her half dead, surely a nearly drowned person could not look beautiful? Then she had been muffled in his over-large clothes with no make-up to disguise the ravages of her ordeal, nor had she dared to ask him to buy cosmetics for her.

'Is that the way you usually receive compliments?' he teased. 'Surely you must know you're exceptionally good-looking.'

'But ... but you must know so many lovely and

sophisticated women with whom I can't compare.
You've only seen me looking a mess.'

'You couldn't look a mess, as you put it, nor do I
care for artificial aids to beauty. But my prefences aren't
the point. Your fairness would make you seem like a
fairy princess to a dark Greek and you were certainly
showing all you'd got. Corfiote boys mature early.'

'Aren't you making mountains out of molehills?'
she asked. In spite of herself she felt flattered, but she
was sure he was exaggerating her effect upon Dion. 'I
wasn't expecting Dion and he caught me unawares,
but really he didn't think anything of it after the first
surprise.'

Cass's well-shaped mouth curled satirically. 'Are you
really such an innocent, Rachel? If you displayed yourself on Simonides' yacht as you did in my kitchen I'm
not surprised you had to jump into the sea.'

Sidetracked by the mention of her enemy, she asked
apprehensively: 'Was there any sign of the *Nausicaa* in
Corfu?'

'I didn't go as far as Corfu, there are shops in nearer
places!' He moved towards her menacingly. 'May I
have your assurance that you'll behave more discreetly
in future?'

Rachel was more annoyed than intimidated; Cass's
attitude towards Dion was like a hen with one chick.
She regarded him scornfully out of eyes that had gone
all emerald and her body assumed an unconsciously
challenging stance as she said coolly:

'If you mean by that I'm to snub Dion if we meet
again, I emphatically won't. I liked the boy and he
liked me ...'

She got no further, with a sudden swoop Cass caught
her round the waist in an iron grip, and his grey eyes

gleamed like molten silver. Involuntarily it occurred to her that it was not only the Greek boy who had been excited by her innocent nudity.

'You will do as I say.'

'Or else?' she enquired sweetly. 'You're behaving like the villain in a melodrama, Cass. What would your girl-friend think of *your* behaviour?'

'Shut up,' he said rudely, drawing her within the circle of his arms. 'Yanni was right, you're a siren or a sea witch. I can't resist that mouth.'

The kiss was long and lingering and it affected Rachel as no such salute had ever done before. Naturally Cass was experienced, and knew how to arouse her. Against her will she found herself responding to his caressing hands. Her heart was beating madly against her ribs and her bones seemed to be melting. In every fibre of her being she was conscious of his hard lean body pressed against her own, the contact of his equally hard mouth, his lips forcing hers apart. Finally when she began to feel faint, he pushed her away from him. She sought the edge of the table to support herself and they stared at each other blankly, both breathing hard.

Slowly Rachel's racing pulses returned to normal and she lifted a hand to her bruised lips.

'You're a nice one to talk about seducing Dion, Caspar Dakers,' she said contemptuously. 'What do you think you're playing at?' She straightened herself, lifting her head proudly. 'Don't you ever dare to touch me again!'

But her brave façade crumbled as the realisation of her helplessness swept over her. She was alone with only this unpredictable man to help her and he was proving as great a danger as the brute from whom she had fled. She turned away with a half sob, staring blindly at the greenery beyond the window.

A faint compunction showed on the man's face. It was only a flicker and was gone. He thrust his hands into his trouser pockets and smiled cynically.

'I'm afraid that was bound to come to you sooner or later,' he told her. 'Don't tell me you've never been kissed before.'

With an effort she rallied. 'Of course, but there are degrees in kissing. Do you consider yourself an expert?'

'Well, what would you say?'

'That I'm sorry for your girl-friend if she believes you're serious about her.'

He looked at her oddly. 'That's something I prefer not to discuss with you. I apologise for behaving like a boor, but you're so provocative.'

'I don't mean to be.'

'Then it must come natural to you.' He was scrutinising her closely, from gilded hair to rope-sandalled feet, as if every detail of her appearance had some significance for him. 'You stir ... memories.'

She looked at him enquiringly, but he said no more. Moving over to the window, he stood staring out with unseeing eyes. The sunlight glittered on the glossy leaves of the shrubs massed beneath it, a gorgeous butterfly spread on one of the blooms. In the silence that followed, the click of the cicadas and the hum of bees was clearly audible. In the clear light Cass's face was strongly etched, straight nose, arrogant chin and the slanting eyes and brows which gave him a slightly satanic look. They were a legacy from his Magyar mother and made him appear alien. Vaguely Rachel wondered what she had been like.

Without turning his head, he drew a hand across his

brow as if sweeping away some unwelcome recollection, and told her:

'I once knew a girl very like you.'

If this was meant to be an explanation of his behaviour, it seemed to Rachel to be a little inadequate. He must have known a great many girls and it was not strange that one of them should have had a likeness to herself.

'That's adding insult to injury,' she said tartly. 'I'm not even original, merely a substitute for an unfulfilled dream.'

He started at her words, which apparently were more apt than she knew.

'That's truer than you realise,' he returned heavily. He moved away from the window and his sombre glance swept over her. 'I'm afraid I misjudged you because of her.'

'From which I gather she wasn't a nice girl?'

He shrugged his shoulders. 'Nice is an insipid word and certainly didn't apply to her. But she was lovely ...' He sighed. 'I was a raw youth and didn't know how to deal with her.' A cruel glint came into his eyes. 'I would now, and I'd have no mercy.'

A vengeful character, Rachel thought. For the woman's sake I hope he never does meet her; but it had hardly been fair to take out his frustration upon her.

'But that's past history,' he went on. 'Shall we do the washing up?'

It seemed such a prosaic suggestion after the emotion-fraught moments that had just passed, and Rachel laughed.

'Don't you bother,' she told him, aware of a lightening atmosphere. 'You must have arrears of work after having spent the morning shopping on my behalf. I'll do it—and don't forget to make a note of what I owe you for the clothes.'

'I don't feel I can concentrate,' he complained. 'You're a disturbing influence, Rachel.'

'Now you're making me feel guilty.'

'You *are* guilty.' He walked towards the door into the hall. He had a long supple stride and watching him, Rachel was conscious of how very attractive he was. If he made further advances she doubted if she would have the resolution to resist him, even though she knew she was only a stand-in for a lost love. She caught her breath as she realised where her thoughts were tending and became very busy with the dishes in the sink.

At the door Cass turned about giving her a long considering look, a slumbrous, sensuous look that as she caught it, caused her heart to quicken its beat.

'Are you really innocent, Rachel?'

She nodded as she put a plate in the draining rack, half ashamed to have to confess her lack of experience.

'Rare in this day and age,' he commented wonderingly. 'But you're not frigid.' Rachel blushed as she recalled her surrender in his arms. 'Sooner or later you'll take the plunge. Perhaps you've a husband in view and are keeping yourself for him?'

'Actually I haven't, but I've always considered casual lovemaking rather cheap,' she said primly.

'I see,' he drawled. 'But perhaps you could be persuaded to change your mind?'

She threw him a half-frightened glance, then a defence occurred to her.

'Not by an engaged man, it wouldn't be fair,' she said firmly.

'Have I said I was engaged?'

'You implied it. Perhaps you haven't got as far as that yet?'

He grinned mischievously. 'That's my business, but don't be afraid, I've no intention of taking advantage of your situation, so you won't need to jump into the sea again, though I fancy you'd find me preferable to Panos Simonides.'

Rachel drew a deep breath. He was playing with her, but it was not a game she enjoyed. He would know from her involuntary response to him that there was a favourable chemical reaction between them. At least she concluded he had sensed it too. She had felt none of the revulsion which Simonides' proximity awoke in her. But it would be disastrous for her to yield to his lure, for she was not the type who can take such affairs lightly, and Cass had had far too many. She feared he was regarding her as an attractive diversion fate had thrown in his way, and was undeterred by fidelity to the girl he meant to marry. He would say, as he had told her, his deviations were none of her business.

He had confessed that she, Rachel, reminded him of a former love, who it seemed had treated him badly, and possibly his anger over the Dion episode had its root in a forgotten jealousy. That girl had been a flirt and he had revenged himself for her defection upon her unoffending self. Because her prototype had been flighty he doubted her own morals. The likeness was an unfortunate coincidence, she thought ruefully, and put her in a vulnerable position. Somehow she would have to convince him she was virtuous, for she did not put much reliance upon his statement that he would not exploit her situation.

Meanwhile he seemed to expect an answer to his question, for he was regarding her quizzically without making any move to go.

'Your outer seeming may be an improvement upon Panos's,' she told him coolly, 'but basically you want the same thing. Please understand, Mr Dakers, that I'm not available to him, Dion or any other man.'

'Bravo!' he laughed mockingly. 'Now I know where I stand. As I told you, you needn't worry, my dear, I've no use for victims. While you're in my house your person will be sacrosanct, unless you have a change of heart.'

The door closed upon his exit and Rachel proceeded with the washing up. She was wondering uneasily if she had not fallen out of the traditional frying pan into the fire, and a very hot fire too, for she doubted if she could maintain aloof indifference towards Cass Dakers. She could only hope that they would soon have news that the *Nausicaa* had left the vicinity and she could proceed on her way leaving him behind for ever.

CHAPTER FOUR

CASPAR DAKERS spent the afternoon in his writing room, which was on the opposite side of the house to Rachel's. There came muted through his closed door the rattle of his typewriter. The bungalow only comprised four rooms and she hoped he had spoken the truth and it did not inconvenience him to give up the bedroom.

She lay on the bed through the hottest hours of the day, the time when Mediterranean peoples take their siestas, in a half doze, for she was still tired from the ordeal of the day before and the upset of the morning had not helped to restore her.

About four o'clock she got up and took a shower. Rummaging in the bathroom cupboard she discovered an unused hairbrush and was able to give her hair the grooming it needed. She had neglected to ask Cass to buy her one. There was no sound from his room, the typewriter was silent and she wondered if he had gone out while she had been resting.

She went into the living room and gazed wistfully out of the window. The sinking sun flooded the country with golden light, lengthening the shadows. The sea was emerald and purple, the long tongues of rock that ran out into it bone-white in contrast. Rachel was longing for a swim, but even the terrace was forbidden her.

She did not hear Cass come in and started violently at the sound of his voice asking for a cup of tea.

'Your nerves seem on edge,' he remarked as she turned to face him, her eyes wide and fearful.

'You startled me,' she explained, recovering herself. 'I didn't know anyone was there.'

In the bright light her head shone like burnished metal, and his eyes strayed over it almost with apprehension.

'I'll get that tea,' she said hurriedly, and went past him into the kitchen.

He followed her and took out the cups and saucers while she put the kettle on. She cut some bread and butter and he produced a tin of biscuits. There was a domestic intimacy about the proceedings as if they were relatives or husband and wife. He threw covert glances in her direction, noting her deft practised movements, though he did not speak, but there was no constraint between them.

'Couldn't I go for a swim?' she asked as she poured boiling water into the teapot, and as he frowned added, 'The villagers must know I'm here, Dion will have told them.'

'Dion will not have told them, he obeys orders,' said Cass. 'And Yanni for his own reasons will keep quiet about that expedition. Anyway, he'll have expected you to have disappeared by now.'

'Vanished into thin air?'

'Exactly, since he declared you were a nereid, as I told you. He's very superstitious. There are quite a lot of legends about those creatures, some of which you'll find in one of my books. And I must say you look like one.'

Rachel sighed. Ignoring the personal allusion, she said, 'I wish I knew Greek and could talk to the real

Corfiotes. I mean the country people, not the ones who cater for tourists.'

'I could teach you, it would give you something to do.'

She shook her head. 'Hardly worth while starting as I shan't be here long. I suppose you haven't heard anything?'

Which she realised was a stupid question as he had not been out of the house, but he answered seriously:

'Not a whisper, they're possibly still searching. It takes a little time for the sea to wash up a body and it could come ashore anywhere in the bay between Kassiope and Corfu Town, or even in Albania.'

'Ugh!' Rachel shivered as she poured out his cup of tea. The connotation was unpleasant. Cass took the tea, putting in four lumps of sugar from the bowl he had put on the table, and stirred it absently. His aquiline face had a remote brooding look. Rachel surmised that he was still lost in whatever he had been writing. She poured out her own tea while eyeing him furtively. He was quiet and looked a little stern, quite a different person from the angry man she had encountered earlier in the day.

'I'm afraid you must be content to confine yourself to the house,' he told her almost gently. 'There are plenty of magazines and periodicals in the living room.'

Her eyes went to the greenery outside the window.

'It seems such a shame to stay indoors when it looks so glorious outside,' she complained.

His mouth twitched. 'It was your idea to seek sanctuary here,' he pointed out.

'And I'm not ungrateful for your hospitality.'

He smiled quizzically.

'Given under protest. All right, my dear,' as she was

about to speak, 'I've become reconciled to your presence. We shall just have to bear with each other, shan't we?' He sat down on the edge of the table dangling one foot. 'How about some omelettes for supper? There are plenty of eggs.'

'I thought you didn't care for messes, as you called them. Wouldn't you prefer roast beef?' She had noticed a joint in the freezer.

'I don't think there is any, only a ham which you can deal with another day. It's too hot for warm food, and if my lady cook will oblige I fancy an omelette.'

She flushed a little, for his eyes were mischievous, and answered briskly.

'Then omelettes it shall be. Of course I'll pay you for my keep while I'm here.'

'On the contrary, it's customary to pay cooks for their services ... or is it a labour of love?'

There was such meaning in the look that accompanied his last phrase that her flush deepened.

'None of that,' she said sharply, aware of a stab of excitement. There was something about Cass which provoked her in spite of her determination to keep their relationship impersonal.

'That was not a *double entendre*,' he informed her coolly. 'Can it be that you're allergic to love?'

'Depends what you mean by love. Real love is ennobling, sexual love is often a euphemism for something else.'

'Dear me, what a scathing comment!' He stood up and stretched. 'I must get back to work. I like to have my supper about seven when it's cool.'

'Okay, sir.'

His eyes narrowed. 'I don't want any impertinence, Miss Reed.'

'That wasn't impertinence, it was a precise summing up of our situation, Mr Dakers.'

'I stand corrected.' His mocking gaze slid over her, critically assessing her appearance, from her shining head to her rope sandals. The green outfit suited her boyish slenderness, the trousers emphasising the length of her legs.

'I chose the right colour for you,' he decided with satisfaction.

'Rachel, who was sitting on a stool at the table, became engrossed in the bottom of her tea-cup, ignoring this comment.

'Do you see your future in the tea-leaves?' he enquired. 'I'm sure it's an adventurous one.'

'No, I can't tell fortunes and I think I'd rather not know what's coming,' she said with a quiver in her voice. 'Unpleasantness is bad enough when it happens without anticipating it.'

'And you're so sure your future won't be happy?'

'The odds are against it,' she returned.

It would take a long time to erase the hurt done by the one being upon whom she had the greatest claim. When she returned to England she would be quite alone in the world and all she could hope for was a position as a cook or a cook-general to enable her to make a living. Fortunately that profession was not overcrowded.

Cass regarded her downcast face noting the sad droop of her lips.

'Cheer up,' he said more kindly than he had yet spoken. 'Things often turn out better than expected. I must do some more work now, but tomorrow we can have a picnic on Pantokrator.' Rachel flashed him a look of surprise, and he explained, 'We're unlikely to meet·

anyone up there except a few shepherds who won't know who we are. It's hard on you being cooped up all day, and the mountain is less populous than the sea. Will that please you?'

The sparkle returned to her mobile face.

'It would be wonderful,' she exclaimed. 'You are kind, Cass.'

His long mouth curled satirically.

'You can get that idea out of your head, my girl. My motives are never kind.'

'I don't believe it,' she declared energetically. 'You merely consider it weak or cissy or something absurd to admit to kindness.'

'Keep your illusions if they please you,' he told her carelessly. 'In this case I happen to like roaming up mountains and I can put up with your company for once, you can carry the food. Adìo.'

He raised his hand in mock salute and sauntered out of the room.

Rachel cleared the tea things, smiling to herself. Caspar Dakers had a reputation to maintain for being a cynic. The image he wanted to present to the world was as hard and bright as a diamond—that was the reason for his caustic comments and his assault upon herself. He wanted her to think he was a hardbitten man of the world who respected nobody. But he had jumped into the sea to pull her out of it at some risk to himself, and had brought her to his house fearing the rough peasants who did not know her language might frighten her. Though her presence might prove detrimental to him, especially if his fiancée learned of it, he had not thrown her out, and now, sensing her feeling of captivity he had suggested this outing on the morrow to relieve it.

She felt a little glow of triumph that she had come to know him so much better than his critics did. They would not credit him with the kind or disinterested motives she was sure she had discovered in him. Naturally she must play along with him, pretend an indifference she did not feel, accept his sarcasm, even his kisses with equanimity, and make herself useful in any way she could. She was confident he would make no attempt to seduce her, but he talked as if he would because that was his pose. He had a reputation for being a devil with women that for some reason he wanted to preserve, but like many such reputations it was exaggerated. It flattered his ego, which at some time must have been wounded, for she had deduced that there had been a painful episode in his youth with a silver-gilt blonde which had caused him to resent her because she resembled his early love and reminded him of her. It was a pity she was not a brunette, she reflected whimsically; blondes always seemed suspect, though surely Delilah, that prototype of feminine treachery, must have been dark.

Rachel summoned him to supper before she actually cooked the omelettes, for to be at their best they must be served straight out of the pan. Over the meal he questioned her more closely about her plans. Once she was assured that Panos Simonides had left Ionian waters, she proposed to fly to Britain, but what then? Had she relations to whom she could go? Any prospect of employment?

'Or have you a private income?'

She did not resent his questions, believing they were put out of genuine concern for her welfare. He was not taunting her now, but was serious, even grave as he watched her, noticing the despondent look on her expressive face as she contemplated a bleak future.

'No, I've only a few pounds in the bank,' she admitted frankly. 'But it's enough to keep me going for a week or two. I've had an expensive but mainly useless education, and I'm not qualified for anything. I did, however, learn to cook because I like cooking. I shall find a job all right.'

He looked at her slim tapering hands which bore no sign of toil.

'You're contemplating a position as a domestic servant?' he asked incredulously.

'Help, we don't call them servants nowadays!'

'Another euphemism. They serve others, don't they?'

'What's wrong with that? We're all servants to somebody. You serve your public, don't you?'

'You're prevaricating. You'll be bullied and exploited.'

'Oh no, I shan't. I know my worth. Have you ever eaten a better omelette?'

'The men in the house will try to seduce you,' he warned.

'Didn't you have a shot at that yourself?'

He had the grace to look slightly ashamed at this reminder of his violence over Dion. Then his face hardened and he said coldly:

'That should warn you what to expect.'

'I know how to protect myself.'

Only she had not, she had nearly swooned in his arms, but it was very unlikely that she would meet another Cass.

'Do you?' He grinned wickedly. 'In that case you wouldn't mind stopping here?'

Rachel stared at him blankly.

'But I thought you wanted to be rid of me?'

'That was before I'd sampled your culinary skill.'

'But ... but ...' She was bewildered by this change of front. 'Your reputation, your friends, your girl-friend.' She reiterated all the reasons he had brought forward against hiding her in his house.

'Surely a lone bachelor is entitled to employ a house-keeper?' he said plaintively. 'Of course I won't allow you to work in my kitchen in a bathing suit. You must be suitably dressed, an overall or some such.'

The narrow grey eyes were simmering with mis-chief and he gazed at her as if he were recalling the sight of her bare limbs that had so incensed him when he had caught her with Dion.

His sensuous expression caused her to move un-easily.

'I thought for a moment you were serious,' she said, forcing a laugh.

'But I am, perfectly serious. A few months in Corfu would do you good. It's a beautiful island, but I must insist you keep away from Dion.'

That annoyed her; it was unnecessary to keep harp-ing upon what had been a totally harmless incident. He could not have made more fuss if he had caught them embracing; as it was, he was the one who had done that.

'I'm not a cradle-snatcher,' she declared angrily.

'He's nearly as old as you are,' Cass informed her, 'but I know young girls often prefer ... riper fruit.'

There was such meaning in his glance that she caught her breath.

'I wouldn't dare to work for you.'

'Chicken, eh? But I'm not Simonides, I don't de-bauch my employees,' he said scornfully, and Rachel wilted.

'I ... I didn't mean that.'

'Then what's biting you?' She was silent; she did not know how to take him. She had decided that the image he presented to the world was a false one, and that fundamentally he was generous and kindly, which meant that unless she was mistaken he was worthy of her trust. To stay on in Corfu was a very tempting prospect and a solution of her problems. But the looks he gave her from time to time and his frequent innuendoes made her feel uncomfortable and though she did not flatter herself that such a brilliant man could find her attractive, she was conscious of electricity sparking between them during their exchanges. It might be all upon her side but it would not make for a peaceful co-existence. Peace was essential to her now, to lick her wounds and re-orientate her life, and this lovely corner of Corfu was ideal for healing and reflection, but it would be a useless exercise if her emotions were going to be affected by this most disturbing personality.

Cass was watching her with a little derisory smile and she had an uncanny feeling that he knew what was passing in her mind. That was the danger, he was much too astute.

'You're approaching the proposition from the wrong angle,' he told her. 'Trying to read emotional complications into it which don't exist. What you ought to be considering is how much you dare ask in the way of salary, or rather how much I'll pay you. This will be a business contract. Of course it'll all have to be sub rosa, as you can only stay here as a visitor officially. But later on, if we're both satisfied with each other, and you'd like to make it a permanency, you could apply for a work permit, and ...'

'Oh, stop, stop!' she interrupted, putting her hands over her ears to shut out the sound of his voice, half persuasive, half mocking. 'It's impossible, Mr Dakers, and you know it is.'

'I don't know it. Surely you're not so old-fashioned as to have conventional qualms? You didn't have a chaperone on Simonides' yacht, did you?' Rachel started guiltily and he took her expression for confirmation. 'Incidentally, you told me you were engaged to do secretarial work. Now you say your only skill is cooking.'

The last thing Rachel wanted was an enquiry into her status on the *Nausicaa*. To say she had been engaged as a secretary had been a blunder, for she could not type. She sought to cover up by saying hurriedly,

'I'm a better cook than typist.'

She knew he had a typewriter in his work room and hoped desperately that it would not occur to him to ask her to use it on his behalf when her ignorance would be revealed. If he did she would have to pretend an injury to her hand, and she loathed pretence. Because hers was an honest nature, she had an impulse to confide in him, to tell him the whole miserable truth, but he might find her story so fantastic he would not believe it and she shrank from confessing how she had allowed herself to be imposed upon.

To her relief he probed no further.

'I'll leave you to think it over,' he said lightly. 'English summers aren't a patch upon those in Corfu and you look as though you needed some sunshine.'

'Before we decide anything we need to know what Mr Simonides is doing,' she observed tightly. 'And I'm sure your girl-friend wouldn't approve of the arrangement.'

'She's away,' he told her, absently playing with the stem of his wine glass. He had opened a bottle of retsina to accompany their meal, which Rachel privately thought tasted like varnish. He glanced at her enigmatically. 'Until we're married, she's no right to criticise my choice of housekeepers. Most people on the island employ Greek girls, and very handsome they are too, nobody thinks anything of it.'

The implication was not lost upon her, and she wondered if his lady love had objected to a previous employee and that was why he no longer had a maid.

'Have you sampled them?' she asked pertly.

'Dion's sister "did for me", as they say, for a while and kept the house in order while I was away, but she didn't sleep here, of course. Now she's married and I haven't bothered to replace her. She didn't cook like you do.'

'You haven't had much of it, only a soufflé and an omelette.'

'Ah, but I recognised the expert touch.'

Rachel was puzzled. If he were really serious about his Greek friend, he must surely know she would be incensed by her presence in the house. Without being unduly vain, and heaven knew her looks had brought her so much trouble she could wish she were plain, no fiancée would approve of intimate contact with a girl of her appearance, for she *would* be sleeping in the house and she was not a peasant. Greeks, she had always understood, were jealous, possessive and passionate. Cass must know that and that by employing her he would probably jeopardise his engagement, or near engagement, whatever it was. Or was he banking on the girl's absence and the remoteness of his bungalow to conceal the fact that his new housekeeper was young and fair? A situation that could not continue indefinitely.

'She's bound to get to know,' she warned him.

'Who's bound to know what?'

'You know what I mean.'

'Don't be silly. I'm not asking you to be my mistress but my cook.'

'She'll think it's the same thing,' Rachel said bluntly.

She wondered if perhaps that was what he had in mind after all. It would seem to him perfectly natural, as it would to many girls of her acquaintance, but she had no intention of becoming one of the points in a triangle.

'What nasty minds you women have,' Cass rebuked her mildly. 'I pull a woman out of the sea, discover she's an excellent cook and without visible means of support. Being tired of preparing my own meals, I suggest she stays for a while—out of gratitude, shall we say, for saving her life—to attend to my chores while I complete some important work that's behind schedule. What's wrong with that?'

'You make it sound reasonable,' Rachel admitted, 'but you must allow that you started off on the wrong foot.'

'What do you mean by that?'

'Well, you called me several impolite names and ... er ... kissed me,' Rachel explained. 'So you can't complain if it gave me ideas.'

'How unfortunate!' The narrow eyes gleamed wickedly. 'You see your choice of kitchen wear gave *me* ideas. However, you've convinced me they were mistaken ones, so shall we start again? I promise I won't make any more passes at you.'

Rachel, to her shame and dismay, experienced acute disappointment. She assured herself angrily that of course she did not want any further advances from him; she could only stay with him if their respective attitudes towards each other were impersonal and indifferent. She was far too fastidious to court casual embraces and to desire them from another woman's man was contemptible. She should be thankful for that promise, for at the moment she had nowhere else to go. She said primly,

'Then I'll be happy to stay and work for you, Mr Dakers, but only until I know Mr Simonides presents no further threat. After that I must be on my way. It'll be best for all concerned.'

'You think so, do you? There I disagree. Finding myself on to a good thing, I don't want to lose you, and you'd have a better life here than in a London suburb waiting upon some unpleasant woman's whims.'

'She needn't necessarily be unpleasant,' Rachel pointed out, noticing he had not mentioned the other girl, who surely would have something to say if she stayed on. 'But there isn't any hurry,' she tried to placate him, 'and I'm very grateful for the refuge and ... er ... everything else, Mr Dakers.'

'For God's sake don't Mr me all the time,' he exclaimed irritably. 'Call me Cass, everybody does.'

'Oh no, I couldn't call my employer Cass.'

'Determined to keep me at a distance?'

'Isn't that what you promised?'

'I did, but there's a difference between ... er ... kissing and the formality of surnames.'

'I think it's better so,' she declared firmly. 'Then we won't forget our stations.'

He seemed about to protest, but checked himself.

He looked her up and down ironically, and she looked more like a creature of the woods, slim, tall and green-clad, with her fragile bones and golden plaits, than a prospective domestic.

'Very well,' he agreed, 'but does that preclude our expedition tomorrow? Perhaps you consider that too informal for master and maid?'

'Oh no!' she cried involuntarily, for she was looking forward to going out. Then prudence reminded her that perhaps she was being unwise and she added regretfully, 'It would be more suitable if I stayed at home to mind the house while you're gone.'

'You absurd child,' Cass said indulgently. 'You want to go, so why dream up excuses to deny yourself? Are you a masochist by any chance?' Rachel's eyes widened and he laughed. 'Of course we'll go, and to the devil with suitability.' He subjected her to a long searching look. 'For your comfort, nobody will know anything about it.'

With that sophistry, Rachel soothed her conscience and went to bed filled with eager anticipation.

Cass was up before she was next morning, which made her feel guilty, and she murmured something about an alarm clock.

'Don't possess such a thing,' he told her. 'And I'm always an early riser. Don't worry, you're in time to get the breakfast.'

While she prepared bacon and eggs—he confessed he liked an 'English' breakfast—he packed the worn knapsack he produced with food for their picnic. Then when they were seated, he handed her the local paper which had been delivered before she was awake, indicating a small paragraph. It stated that Panos Simonides, the well-known shipping magnate, had called at Corfu on his way to Athens and he and his guests had been entertained by the governor and watched a cricket match before he continued his journey in the late evening. There was no mention of a missing passenger.

'So he decided to cut his losses,' Cass said drily.

The print wavered before Rachel's eyes and she felt sick. Nobody on that yacht had cared that she was probably drowned, or had made enquiries about her possible survival. The passengers had gone to a cricket match and then continued on their voyage as if she had never existed.

Noticing her stricken look, Cass put his own interpretation upon it.

'So your vanity is wounded,' he suggested silkily. 'You're devastated to discover Simonides put so little value upon his missing secretary.'

'I couldn't care less about his actions,' Rachel said dully. 'But he wasn't the only person on board upon whom I had a claim.'

'Aha!' Cass exclaimed triumphantly. 'The plot thickens. So there was a knight errant among the crew whom you expected to comb the island for you? But I don't suppose the poor devil would have much chance to do that if Simonides put his veto on it. He evidently wants to avoid trouble.'

Rachel pushed her plate with its slice of half eaten toast away.

'There was nobody like that,' she told him quietly. 'But it seems so callous.'

'The Simonides of this world are completely callous,' Cass remarked, watching her white face curiously. It was obvious she had received a blow; she had expected someone to enquire for her.

'Don't despair,' he went on, 'Simonides wouldn't want to publicise your loss since it might lead to queries derogatory to his character, but he will have left instructions with private agents to conduct a discreet search.'

The sudden panic in her eyes indicated that he was on the wrong track.

'So I'm not safe yet.'

Cass grinned reassuringly. 'I don't suppose they'll exert themselves to pursue their enquiries very far. They'll tell Simonides that you must be presumed drowned since there are no reports of a body being found.'

Rachel laughed a little shakily. 'It's rather weird to be alive when presumed dead. I feel as if I were a ghost.'

And she looked like one, for all the colour had left her face and her big eyes had darkened with a haunted look.

'Can't you confide in me?' Cass asked gently, since it was obvious she was concealing something. 'I can keep a secret.'

Again Rachel was tempted to do so, but Cass was after all a very worldly man, and might take the view that she had been a fool. Simonides was a very wealthy man and she had missed a chance to milk him through her fastidiousness. In his writing he had proclaimed that all women were venal and he was hardly likely to consider she was an exception, especially as she had told him she was without friends or funds. He would consider she had acted like an irresponsible little idiot and have no understanding of her sense of abandonment. In any case it was all behind her now, the last tie had been sundered.

'There's no secret,' she said stonily. 'I've merely been

disillusioned.' She forced a laugh. 'A common occurrence in human relationships.'

'You couldn't have had any illusions about Simonides,' Cass declared. 'One look at the fellow would have told you what he was.'

Rachel shuddered. 'Let's forget it,' she said wearily. It was not Simonides she had been thinking about. 'But if I'm still being sought, I can't leave yet, so if your offer is still open I'll be glad to accept it ... temporarily.'

'I thought you had accepted it,' Cass observed. 'And I hope I can persuade you to make it permanent, since you've no friends or relations apparently to object.'

Rachel's eyes filled with tears at this reminder that the only kin she had did not care whether she was dead or alive.

'For God's sake don't cry,' Cass exclaimed in alarm. 'There's no reason why your stay here shouldn't be a pleasant if not a happy one.'

His unexpected concern was balm to her wounded spirit. He had changed since the previous day when she had had to plead with him to shelter her. Another thought occurred to her.

'You couldn't get into trouble for letting me stay here?' she asked anxiously, for that would be a poor repayment for his hospitality.

'Why should I? In any case, if any official comes asking questions I'll tell him I found you on the beach suffering from amnesia and you've only just remembered who you are.'

She smiled wanly and wiped her eyes.

'I'm being a terrible imposition.'

'My dear girl, my house is yours, as the Spanish say, and you know I need your culinary services.'

'You're very good,' she told him gratefully. 'But

would the authorities believe your story about the amnesia?'

'Why shouldn't they if I sound convincing? After all, making up stories is my trade. Now don't waste any more grief over old Bluebeard's lack of concern for you and come out into the sunshine. Mount Pantokrator awaits us.'

His reference to Simonides told her that he still suspected she was having regrets on his account, but she would rather he thought that than that he knew the truth. He helped her clear up the breakfast things in spite of her protests, saying the sooner they could get off the better before the sun grew too hot. When they were ready, and she lifted the straps of the knapsack to slip about her shoulders, he took it from her and hoisted it on to his own back.

'I wasn't serious about that,' he told her. 'You'll need all your strength to carry your own weight, you still look a bit frail.'

'Oh, I'm fine and equal to anything,' she assured him, and they stepped out into the bright morning.

Rachel's spirits rose, for this one day she would leave all her problems and griefs behind her. That the biggest of them might be walking beside her did not occur to her.

CHAPTER FIVE

THEIR way lay up a cleft in the mountainside, an ascending valley filled with trees, which thinned as they approached its upper end. A narrow track wound through it which they followed one behind the other. Cass strode in front to indicate the route with the confident tread of one who was familiar with the terrain. He had cut himself a stout stave from amid the undergrowth, not, he told Rachel, because he feared an attack by savage natives, but to ward off the dogs that protected their owners' property and were sometimes over-enthusiastic about their duty. As the very few dwellings they sighted were very isolated, Rachel did not blame them. When they did come across a small shack in a clearing, mangy curs barked to announce the approach of strangers, but none molested them. The huts, they were little more, were occupied by black-clad women who called a greeting, their menfolk being out in the woods or down by the sea. Cass seemed to be a familiar figure to them, and he responded with a few words in the Greek patois as he went past.

Sometimes the path was so steep and rocky it was more like climbing than walking, but Rachel, in spite of her fragile looks, was nimble and wiry. At the Swiss school which she had attended when her formal education was completed, she had ridden, swum and played tennis to an extent which had worried her governesses, who feared she would damage her complexion or her figure, which they considered to be the most important assets a girl possessed. It was not until she left, and spent her nineteenth year in her mother's society, that she realised what had been the finishing school's aim. She was being trained, as were her fellow students, all of them daughters of wealthy parents, to attract a rich husband and be capable of entertaining his friends. Though Desirée grumbled at the high fees, she regarded them as an investment. Rachel could look higher than poor Angus Reed, and with her looks should be able to capture an affluent husband who would also be a prop to his charming mother-in-law's declining years.

Rachel viewed the prospect with disfavour. She did not want to marry unless she fell in love, and she disliked the fast jet set with which her mother mingled on the strength of her last alimony, whenever she was out of a job, and engagements became less and less frequent. In vain she begged her parent to allow her to train for a profession that would allow her to earn her own living and be independent. Desirée had scoffed at such aspirations.

'You don't know what you're talking about,' she had told her daughter. 'You wouldn't enjoy struggling along on a pittance. You've been blessed with looks and charm and they'll achieve for you the sort of life that's worth living. I had to come up the hard way, and I didn't enjoy it, but you're there already. I've plans for you, Ray, and if you play your cards right, you and I will spend the rest of our lives in luxury.'

In due course Rachel learned what those plans were.

The contrast between the sort of existence Desirée favoured and her present surroundings was almost ludicrous. What her mother spent in six months would have kept these peasant families in plenty for several

years. Yet, as Rachel plodded in Cass's wake, she knew
which she would choose. Here were honesty, courage
and brave achievement, while there she had been
smothered in pretensions, insincere flattery and lies.
'Poor little rich girl,' she thought contemptuously, but
that was the irony of it. Desirée was not really well off,
she lived perpetually in debt, debts which she hoped
her daughter's husband would eventually pay for her.

The trees became sparse as they reached the head of
the valley. Pantokrator is not a big mountain as mountains go, being only about nine hundred feet above sea
level, but it is the highest point on Corfu island. It is
not difficult to climb, but Cass had no intention of trying to reach the summit. It would require, he told
Rachel, far too much effort on a hot day. He was aim-
ing for the bare reaches of rocks and scrub above the
treeline from which they would have a panoramic view
of the island. There were no roads after the village of
Spartylas in the south and Kassiope along the coast, so
only a few energetic walkers reached it on foot.

At the top of the cleft, where it merged into the
mountain, Cass came to a halt. Pantokrator's rounded
summit rose above them, behind them were the waving
masses of trees, the green of oak, the silvery-grey of
olive and the occasional dark spire of a cypress, between
them and the sea. A depression in the ground on one
side of them sheltered an olive grove, a patch of vines,
and a few stony fields. In the midst of this small holding
was a stone cottage flanked by an outhouse, surrounded
by a garden bright with flowers, protected by a wattle
fence from the goats, pigs and chickens roaming around
it. A tethered donkey lifted up its voice and brayed a
welcome to them. The place had the appearance of a

THE GARDEN OF THE GODS

prosperous little farm, and the profusion of flowers was unusual.

'Thirsty?' Cass asked, and without waiting for her reply and she was longing for a drink, he went on, 'We'll get old Eileen to give us a glass of orange juice, she's an old pal of mine.'

'Eileen?' Rachel queried. 'That isn't a Greek name.'

'Nor is she Greek, she's Irish. It was quite a romance. She fell for a Greek waiter in Belfast and he, poor soul, was pining to get back home. They both worked hard to earn their passage money and start housekeeping. A bit of luck came along in the form of a small legacy from an aunt, and Eileen bought this place. Georgios had been worried as to how his family would receive an alien bride, but that settled all their worries. In the Greek tradition the wife's dowry provides the home. She's lived here ever since, though Georgios is dead.'

As he related this story, Cass was walking towards the farm. At the gate between the wattle fence, he called:

'Eileen mavourneen, you have visitors!'

The door of the house opened and an old woman came out. Her brown face was seamed with wrinkles, and her white hair straggled from the handkerchief tied round her head. She wore a black skirt and shawl, the uniform of a Greek widow, but her bright shrewd eyes were blue.

'Is it yourself, Caspar Dakers?' she cried in a voice that still retained its Irish lilt. 'I wager you'll be wanting a sup of my special orange juice. Come in, come in and the colleen as well.'

Cass opened the gate and signed to Rachel to precede him. They followed the old woman through the house to a stone porch at the back of it up which grew a wistaria, still in bloom, the mauve flowers and feathery foliage festooning the pillars of the porch. In its shade was a wooden bench and a small round table, evidently home-made.

'Sit yourselves down,' Eileen bade them. 'You're more than welcome. I'll bring your drink and then you can tell me the news of London Town.'

They sat down on the bench, glad to rest after their long walk. As their hostess departed, Rachel looked at Cass reproachfully.

'I thought you didn't want me to meet anybody?'

'Eileen Stavros is no gossip, and few people come up here. You look in need of refreshment and we're very old friends. She'll probably think you're my intended.'

'Then I hope you'll disabuse her,' Rachel said hastily as he shot her a mischievous look.

'I certainly shan't. Oh come, Rachel, a little masquerade won't hurt you and she'll be delighted.'

'But ... but when I go away?'

'Engagements can be broken off, can't they? She may never learn the truth, for I don't often come this way nowadays. There was a time when she was the only person whose company I could tolerate.'

He looked away to the hillside with sombre brooding eyes. Rachel, who had come to associate him with success in all his undertakings, wondered what could have occurred to drive him to seek solace from the ancient Irishwoman.

'She's a comforting person in trouble,' Cass went on. 'Perhaps I should have brought you here in the first place, but it's a long rough path for a half-drowned mermaid.'

'It's certainly a marvellous hideout,' Rachel agreed, 'but I'm glad you didn't.'

He turned his head to look at her intently.

'You are? I thought you regarded me as a cross between a disagreeable gaoler and a reprobate.'

About to deny this description vehemently, Rachel was forestalled by the reappearance of Eileen Stavros carrying a tray on which were two tall thick-bottomed glasses containing orange juice and two little dishes each holding a spoonful of preserve as was the Greek custom. Having served them, she brought out a stool from the inner room and sat down facing them, eyeing them benevolently.

'So at last you've found yourself a bride,' she said to Cass.

'Better late than never,' Cass returned with a glint in his eyes.

Rachel was glad that she had been warned of a possible misunderstanding, and was thankful she did not even blush.

'Och, you waited a long while, but you've chosen a sweet young lady.' Eileen's blue gaze flickered over Rachel. 'And one who shares your love of nature. Like should mate with like. Though me and my man were of different countries, we both wanted the simple life.'

Rachel reflected that no two people could be more dissimilar than herself and Cass. She wished he was not trying to deceive this simple woman, but realised it was too late to explain the real situation.

'You'll not be finding him easy.' Eileen addressed her directly. 'He's had his own way far too long, you'll need patience and understanding.'

'Oh, I understand him very well.' Rachel darted a

malicious glance at Cass's profile. 'And I'll try to culti-
vate patience.'

'You must let love be your teacher.'

Cass said hurriedly, 'How's the family, Eileen?'

'Both the girls are married now, Moiro's gone to live
in Athens. So now my Georgios can start looking for a
wife. Eh, it's a barbarous country where a lad has to see
his sisters wed and dowered before he can think of himself.'

'An old Greek custom,' Cass explained to Rachel.
'A man is responsible for his sisters until they're married.'

'And dowered,' Eileen supplemented. 'A fine litter
of pigs that was costing us, and the olive harvest. What
will you be bringing to your man, missie?'

Cass laughed merrily. 'Eileen, Eileen, Rachel isn't
Greek. You're forgetting we've different customs in
England.'

'Oh ay, I'm getting old and forgetful,' the Irishwoman murmured. 'Will ye live in London?'

'For part of the year. I have to, you know,' Cass said
glibly. 'But Rachel, like myself, prefers country life, and
we'll escape to Corfu when we can, won't we, darling?'

Rachel could not meet the mockery in his glance.
She muttered something inaudible into her tumbler,
and the old woman eyed her shrewdly.

'She's a mite young for you, Caspar.'

'Time will soon remedy that,' Cass said shortly, as if
displeased. He stood up. 'We must be on our way,
mavourneen. Thank you for the refreshment.' He took
out his pocketbook.

'Put that away, or you'll earn my wrath,' Eileen protested. 'Greek or Irish, I don't sell hospitality.'

Cass gave her a charming smile.

'I know that, but you must buy Georgios a wedding present.' He put some drachma notes down on the table. 'When is it to be?'

'Saints above, you're forgetting the customs of this country. He's got his eyes on a girl, but I haven't approached her father yet. Oh, he'll agree, for Georgios will have this farm when I'm gone, and though he's young to wed, I could do with help in the house.'

'I'm sure you could. Let me know when it's settled, and I hope I'll be asked to dance at the wedding.'

'Sure you will, and your young lady too, and I reckon by then she'll be your wife.' She beamed at them. 'Georgios is his godson,' she said to Rachel.

'And that relationship is much more important in Greece than it is at home,' Cass told her. 'Come on, darling, we must be on our way.'

'Thank you very much,' Rachel said to Eileen, holding out her hand. She wished her heart did not lurch every time Cass called her darling.

Eileen clasped her hand and drawing her towards her, raised herself on tiptoe to kiss her brow. Her lips were very dry.

'Be good to him,' she said. 'He's had some rough times and he needs his own woman. But if you have trouble, alannah, and need a friend, come to me. You'll always be welcome here.'

'Thank you,' Rachel said again, 'I'll remember that.' She thought it was unlikely she would ever see Eileen Stavros again.

'God preserve you,' the old woman said as they went out.

'She meant that,' Cass told her as they walked away from the farm. 'She'd help anyone, and she seems to have taken a fancy to you. She has a heart of gold.'

'Then the more shame on you for deceiving her,' Rachel said tartly, but Cass only laughed.

'To what dark mystery was she referring when she mentioned rough times?' Rachel enquired.

Cass turned back to give her a quizzical look.

'You don't imagine I've reached mature years without a few knocks?' he retorted. 'I wasn't always rich and successful.'

'Oh, I thought she meant an affair of the heart.'

'You would, being a woman,' he said scathingly.

Rachel decided it would be wiser not to probe further as Cass was looking forbidding, and among his numerous affairs it was unlikely any had gone deep enough to drive him to seek solace at this back of beyond.

'How old is Georgios?' she asked, thinking Cass was young to be the godfather of Eileen's son. The boy had been named for his dead father.

'Oh, about eighteen. I was only twenty myself when I assumed responsibility for him.' (Which made him about thirty-eight, Rachel noted.) 'Eileen isn't as old as she looks. Unremitting toil in the sun makes women aged before their time and she hasn't the advantage of beauty parlours.'

They were above the trees and in a world of rock, scrub and heather with occasional furze bushes. They followed a narrow path worn by sheep or goats. Bees hummed, butterflies flew before them, and occasionally a small snake streaked into its hole at their approach. Lizards sunned themselves on rocks, birds fluttered from bush to bush and varied species of wild flowers sought a precarious existence in the dry soil.

For the first time for many days, Rachel was completely happy. All her misgivings and apprehensions had been left behind her in the valleys below. Up here, in this world of blue, fragrant air, suspended it seemed between earth and sky, it was good to be alive, to feel the vigorous young blood coursing through her veins. She could have shouted from sheer exuberance.

Cass was making for a particular spot, and when he came to it he halted. An outcrop of rock protruded from the hillside with an overhanging shelf throwing the earth beneath it into deep shade.

'This is our dining room,' he announced, lowering the knapsack. He then proceeded to gather an armful of dry herbage which he laid over the sandy soil beneath the rock. From the top of his pack he extracted a thin groundsheet, which he spread over it. All his movements were quick and precise, but Rachel was unaware of what he was doing, for she was gazing spellbound at the view laid out below them. They had had their backs to it during the ascent and it was only when she turned about that she beheld it in all its grandeur. The whole sickle-shaped bay that bit into the eastern side of the island was revealed with its surround of green trees and ridges of white rock running out into a purple-blue sea. In the clear air she could see as far as Corfu town and even imagine she could distinguish the squat shapes of the twin forts that guarded its approach from the sea. The water was a mirror reflecting the sky and on the eastern horizon were the dim mauve shapes of mountains.

'Gorgeous, isn't it?' Cass observed. 'But sit down, girl, and rest your weary limbs.'

She turned to him with an enraptured smile.

'You're right, gorgeous is the word, and I couldn't feel weary in this invigorating air.' She glanced up at the bare slopes above them where the vegetation was sparse. 'Is it far to the top?'

'Too far for this old man,' said Cass, grinning. 'This is my limit for today if it isn't yours. You're showing surprising energy, my child.'

'Don't talk as if you were Methuselah,' Rachel protested, sitting down on the seat he had prepared. 'A hill is a challenge. I always want to see what's on the other side.'

'In this case only a lot of sea.' Cass stretched himself beside her. 'I've been all over it and this is the best vantage point. Fortunately certain zones up here are forbidden areas, so walkers are discouraged, but I, being who I am, have a free pass to wander where I will.'

There was a touch of arrogance in the last statement, a reminder that Caspar Dakers was a privileged person.

'I suppose as long as you continue to write flattering accounts of the island no place will be barred to you,' she suggested.

'That's about it,' Cass agreed. 'But cut out the flattery, my descriptions are truthful.'

'I apologise. The truth about this place doesn't need flattery,' Rachel said softly, her eyes still on the view.

She was sitting crosslegged like a contemplative Buddah, having discarded her sunglasses. Her plaits hung over each shoulder, falling over her knees, ropes of pale gold, and her face was rapt. Cass was not looking at the scenery but at her, lying on his side, his head supported on one elbow, with an expression of appreciation. The dark rock behind her threw into relief ner pale pure profile.

'Suppose you unpack the grub,' he suggested lazily after some moments of contemplation. 'I put in a bottle of wine, Italian not Greek, which you'll prefer, and I'm dry.'

Rachel brought herself back to earth with an effort, and opened the rucksack. There was bread and ham, cucumber, cheese and fruit, the bottle and cardboard cups and plates. Cass roused himself to open the wine while she divided the food. Between mouthfuls he discoursed about the country.

'Corfu was for four centuries under Venetian rule,' he told her. 'Italian influence is very marked. It was one of the last bastions against the Ottoman conquerors and was also for a short time under British rule—they introduced cricket. It's the only place in Greece where it's played. Corfu was ceded to Greece in 1864 with the rest of the Ionian Islands. You're not listening.'

Rachel, half way through a peach, smiled apologetically.

'It's too hot for a history lesson.'

'You ought to show some interest in the place that's sheltering you,' he reproved her, refilling her cup.

She shied the pip of her fruit at a marauding wasp, but missed it. 'Oh, I do,' she told him. 'I appreciate it no end—what was it you called it? The Garden of the Gods.'

'Yes, and the gods always picked the best places, but unfortunately the tourists do too, and their invasion is not so beneficial. All those huge hotels, but I suppose they help the economy, and Greece is a poor country without many natural resources. Most of it is pretty barren, that's why they named Corfu, or Kerkyra to give it its correct name, a garden, and it is compared with the Aegean Islands.'

Rachel gave him a provocative glance. Having eaten his fill he lay at ease on the hard ground, his bare, sinewy forearms and half-revealed chest burned almost black by the strong sun, and stray beams penetrating their shelter found odd gleams of copper among his thick dark brown hair.

'Since you're not a native, you might be included among the invaders,' she suggested.

To her surprise he accepted her description. 'Yes, and I suppose I do the island no service by writing about its beauties to attract other aliens.'

She began to collect the debris of their meal.

'You can't stop progress,' she pointed out, 'though it does seem a shame to see so many charming spots commercialised.'

'It becomes more and more difficult to find solitude,' he grumbled.

'Do you always want to be alone?'

'Not at all. From time to time I reside in London. That's a seething anthill, but as an antidote I need periods of isolation to regain strength to face it again.'

'But when you marry?'

'The eternal feminine preoccupation! You can't see a carefree bachelor without wanting to put a noose round his neck.'

She frowned in perplexity. Hadn't he said there was a Greek girl towards whom he had intentions? Perhaps he could not make up his mind to forgo his freedom. She said thoughtfully:

'Being single is all very fine when you're young and vigorous, but when you're getting on in life you need someone to share your memories, or so it seems to me.'

He looked up at her, and in the strong light, his eyes simmered palely between his dark lashes.

'Like today, for instance?' he queried. 'When you're doddering around bent with rheumatism, you'd like a partner to whom to say, Do you recall that gorgeous day on Pantokrator?'

'That's the idea,' she returned, disturbed by his intent gaze. 'I shall remember this all my life.'

'Will you? But it's so impersonal. Now if you and I were wildly in love, it would be a memory to cherish.'

She turned her head away, aware of a subtle undercurrent. 'Naturally it would make it more poignant,' she said stiffly.

'How cool she is!' Cass observed to the blue sky. 'No encouragement to add the ... er ... poignancy.'

'Mr Dakers, didn't we agree that ... er ... under the circumstances, I can only stay with you if we keep our distance?'

'We did. But today is a holiday.'

Rachel drew her legs under her and knelt up facing him, determined to quell effectively any amorous advances. In this position, she was looking down at him, but she was so near that one of her long braids swept his face. He put up a hand and took hold of it.

'Woman, you're a constant provocation.'

'I don't mean to be,' she said quietly. 'I'm afraid you're too susceptible, Mr Dakers. Suppose you tell me about your girl-friend?'

He pulled off the piece of tape that secured her plait, and proceeded to unravel it. The long swathe of silver-gilt hair sprayed over his arm and chest. Without heeding her suggestion, he observed:

'I've only met one other woman with hair like this, the one you resemble.' He picked up a handful of hair. 'She broke my youthful heart.'

'How sad!' Rachel was with difficulty subduing a wave of excitement that their intimacy aroused in her. She tried to draw back, but he held her by her hair.

'It was sad, because she destroyed my illusions about women. Youths can have ideals, you know.'

'You've come a long way since then,' Rachel pointed out. 'The novel of yours I read made fun of idealists.'

'He jests at scars ...' he quoted.

'Yes, but it goes on, "who never felt a wound." Pain should have taught you understanding.'

'What do you know about it, my child philosopher?' He released her hair and lay back. 'Oh, I forgot, the knight errant on the yacht. Has he left a scar?'

Her face changed, all the light went out of it. The yacht was a memory she did not want to recall.

'Yes,' she said. Let him imagine she had left a champion behind her on the *Nausicaa*, for whom she was repining. If he believed she was committed it would be easier to keep him at bay. Again she said:

'Tell me about your girl-friend.'

'Which one?' The narrowed eyes were mocking slits.

'The one who'll be coming back to Corfu, who won't approve of my engagement as your cook.'

'Too bad, isn't it? She'll have to put up with it.'

'Cass, I'd hate to cause friction between you,' Rachel said earnestly.

'You've done that already.' He sat up abruptly. 'Kiss me.'

She froze. 'Certainly not!' She tried to rise to her feet, but he caught a fistful of hair and held it fast.

'Why not? Don't you want to? I'm good at kissing.'

'You're quite an expert, but I'd rather be excused.'

'Don't lie.' He reached for her other plait and with his hands full of her tresses drew her down to him. 'What's the harm? It's a perfect day and a romantic setting. It'll enhance the memory for your old age.'

'Cass, no!' She tried to free herself, but his grasp of her hair was painful. 'I'm not permissive.'

Her heart was beating wildly and her blood was eager

for his embrace, as he well knew. Traitor body, she thought despairingly.

'I don't care what you are,' he returned. 'I want you.'

'Oh, please!' But her protest was weak.

Then she succumbed. After all, there was no great harm in yielding to his lips, and no doubt the other girl knew of his proclivities.

Cass pulled her down on top of him, then rolled over so that she lay imprisoned by his weight. His arms were about her shoulders, and his mouth sought hers. The physical attraction that was between them flared into consuming flame. She heard Cass give a little gasp and he pressed closer. Freeing one hand, he pulled at the neck of her shirt. A violent reaction swept through Rachel with the recollection of other fingers, thick hairy fingers, tearing at the bodice of her evening gown. Revulsion pulsed through her body and she began to struggle fiercely, pushing Cass's face away from hers.

Becoming aware of her frantic rejection, Cass turned over on to his back, leaving her free. He was breathing fast, and his eyes were closed. Rachel huddled against the rock wall behind them, the storm of emotion he had aroused in her subdued by panic. Mechanically she began to replait her loosened hair with shaking fingers.

Without opening his eyes, Cass spoke.

'You've bewitched me, mermaid, but what are you afraid of?'

Without pausing to think she riposted:

'If I'd wanted to be raped I'd have stayed on the *Nausicaa*.'

Cass pulled himself up, protesting:

'It was nothing like that. You wanted me as much as I wanted you. Are you a prude?'

She gave a long sigh and shook her head.

'I'm beginning to hate men.'

Cass studied her for a long while in silence. She had changed from the glowing girl who had enjoyed their picnic. She looked shrunken and vulnerable crouched against the rock, with what little colour she had had drained away and her eyes dark and haunted. He could only conjecture what had happened on the yacht, but it had left a scar that it would take time and patience to eliminate. The compassion for the weak and helpless, which he always sought to suppress as unbecoming to the hardboiled front he wished to present to the world, welled up in him.

Rachel did not look at him, her eyes were fixed unseeingly at the scene in front of her. Bitterly she was reflecting that though so vastly different in outward seeming, fundamentally Cass and Panos were the same.

'I think I must go to Corfu and chance Panos' agents,' she said dully.

'No, you mustn't dream of doing that,' Cass exclaimed quickly. 'You mustn't let me frighten you away.' He smiled wryly. 'I admit I won't find it easy to exist with an attractive woman on a platonic basis, but I can discipline myself at need. I thought you were willing.'

Rachel had recovered her poise, and she too smiled wryly.

'I'm sorry I misled you. As I said, I'm not permissive.'

But he knew her reluctance went far deeper than any conventional scruples.

'There's only one solution to your problems,' he said decisively. 'Since you're obviously in need of care and protection, as the law courts say.'

'You mean I could go to your Greco-Irish friend?'

'I don't, but we could make what you termed a deception reality.'

Rachel's eyes widened incredulously. 'Cass Dakers, you must have taken leave of your senses if you mean what I think you mean!'

'Eileen would say I've come to them at last.' He grinned impishly, keeping his tone deliberately light. 'It was all that talk about lonely old age that did it. I'm proposing, my darling, to make an honest woman of you and secure the permanent services of a good cook.'

Rachel clutched at her reeling senses; one or other of them must have been touched by the sun. She said feebly:

'But, Cass, we've only been together for a couple of days, we don't know each other at all.'

'Does one ever know another person thoroughly? I'm willing to take a chance on you, and we've as much hope of making a go of it as if we'd had a six months' courtship.'

Rachel began to realise that he was in earnest, and she licked her lips nervously. Watching her he added with intention:

'As St Paul says, it's better to marry than to burn.' He saw a moment's panic in her eyes, and went on re-assuringly, 'I don't want to rush you, darling, and we must marry at once to give me the right to protect you, but I'll not ask for anything more until you're ready to give it.'

So he had divined her fear, and at least they knew they were compatible physically. In time that appalling memory would cease to frustrate her. He was showing a gentleness and consideration of which earlier on

she would not have believed he was capable. Her first
reaction was to suspect he had set a trap for her to get
his way with her, but she knew now it had been an un-
worthy thought, though she was certain that when they
had started out that morning such an idea was as far
from his mind as it had been from hers. Something had
changed him, but she did not believe it was Eileen's
conversation.

'Marriage is a very serious matter,' she said uncertainly.

'Oh, very, that's why I've avoided it for so long. Now
I feel it's time I experienced it. After all, modern marriage isn't very durable, and if we find we've made a
mistake we can rectify it.'

Rachel began to laugh. 'What a way to propose!
You should be protesting undying devotion.'

'You wouldn't believe me if I did. Only teenagers
imagine love lasts for ever.'

And Cass was not a teenager, he was a mature man
and surely could not be so crazy as to want to form a
permanent relationship with a girl who was practically
a stranger. Nor was there any question of love between
them. Sexual attraction was not love, she knew that.
She remembered something else.

'What about the Greek girl?' she asked suddenly.

'What Greek girl?'

'The one you're half engaged to.'

He smiled. 'There's no Greek girl. That was a
fabrication to warn you off in case you had designs on
me.'

'Oh!' Her eyes sparkled with indignation. 'What an
unnecessary precaution! The last thing I wanted was
to become involved with you.'

She had used the past tense.

'But you have,' Cass pointed out. 'I suppose it was inevitable from the moment when I saw you lying on deck looking like ... ' He broke off.

Rachel looked at him enquiringly, but he said no more. She suspected that he still cherished tender feelings for the woman with the silver-gilt hair who had, it seemed, let him down. That would account for his subsequent cynicism, but his proposal to herself was sheer quixotry and quite out of character.

'It's a curious thing,' he went on reflectively. 'Men and women are always drawn to the same type, even if their experience with that type has been unfortunate.'

'Then if I'm like someone who wasn't very ... er ... estimable, you should be warned.'

'I'm sure the likeness is only skin deep,' he said firmly. He smiled at her with none of the usual mockery in his eyes. 'My dear, I want to protect you, you're little more than a child and need someone to look after you.'

She was young enough to resent his motive, but it would have stretched the limit of possibility if he had declared he had fallen in love with her.

'I can look after myself,' she muttered rebelliously.

'You know you can't,' he contradicted her, 'or else you wouldn't be here. You'd rather marry me than have to face Simonides, wouldn't you?'

She had already been shaken by the reminder of the hairy brute that Cass had unwittingly recalled, and now a wave of terror engulfed her.

'But Panos is in Athens,' she cried. Her eyes searched his calm face frenziedly. Did Cass know something which he had not told her? Had he lulled her into false security and was the Greek hunting for her?

'He may return,' Cass warned her, and she turned

frightened eyes towards the sea as if she expected to see the *Nausicaa*'s white hull gliding towards her over the blue expanse.

'Oh no!' she breathed.

'Don't look so scared,' Cass said reassuringly. 'He can't touch you while you're with me.'

Suddenly he became for Rachel a bulwark against all that threatened her, a haven from a cruel world. She threw her arms about his neck, clinging to him desperately.

'Marry me soon, Cass, keep me safe,' she whispered with her cheek against his.

He held her tenderly as a father or a brother might; only the tightening of the muscles around his mouth betrayed the restraint he was putting upon himself.

'I'll do just that,' he promised.

CHAPTER SIX

SOMEWHAT to Rachel's surprise and very much to her relief, Cass made no attempt to avail himself of a fiancé's privileges as she had half expected he would. Even after she had flung herself into his arms, he had merely soothed her, kissed her gently and put her from him. It seemed he was anxious to show her that he was a different sort of animal from Simonides.

As they walked down from the mountain, and the descent was quicker and easier than going up, he had outlined his plans. They would fly back to England as soon as he could book a flight, and he would obtain a special licence so that they could be married at once. Then they they would return to Corfu.

'And really get to know each other,' he concluded.

'It'll be a bit late if we find we don't like each other,' Rachel demurred.

'I can't imagine disliking you, and I hope you won't find me objectionable,' he said a little stiffly.

She flashed him a nervous sidelong glance.

'I'm sure I should never do that, but ...' She hesitated. Suppose when he took her in his arms she experienced again that sudden revulsion that was a legacy inherited from Simonides? But he was not like the Greek, he had nothing of Panos' coarse brutality. She was confident that she would eventually conquer that involuntary recoil, especially as she very much wanted to be able to love him. It had been so unexpected, a physical reaction bound up with the terror

and despair that had assailed her on the *Nausicaa*. But
would Cass be patient and understand, or would their
marriage be wrecked before it had begun? It seemed
he had some inkling of her thoughts, for he reiterated
that she must not be scared of him and he could wait.

She thanked him gratefully. 'I'm sure if you'll bear
with me, in time I'll come to love you as you deserve,'
she said earnestly.

He smiled sardonically. 'More than I deserve, I hope,
for I'm no white knight in shining armour, but have my
full share of human weaknesses. But I'll do my best to
make you happy.'

She noticed he did not suggest he might come to love
her, but then Cass Dakers was contemptuous of love.

He would not admit that he could succumb to that
human weakness.

They were both tired when they reached the bungalow in the evening, but Rachel insisted that it was her
duty to prepare a meal. They found Dion had made
another present of fish during their absence. Cass never
locked the door and he had been in and gutted and
filleted his gift as he had done before. It made a tasty
supper without much trouble.

'He's a good lad,' Cass remarked as they ate at the
kitchen table, 'and he'll honour you as the mistress of
my house.'

Something seemed to be troubling him, and
presently he said:

'There are an awful lot of years between us, Rachel.'

'I prefer older men,' she told him candidly. 'They
give a girl more confidence.'

'With their ability to support and protect?' he suggested, his eyes glinting. 'When I'm past it, you can
always walk out on me. I shan't blame you.'

Rachel was shocked. 'I'd never do that,' she cried vehemently. 'It wouldn't be fair.'

'Fairness be damned!' he exclaimed forcibly. 'I loathe martyrs. Never feel you're tied to me by duty, Rachel, I'd hate that.'

'But if we have children?'

He looked startled. 'Do you want a baby?'

'Don't you?'

'I hadn't really considered it. This has all happened rather suddenly.' He looked at her with laughter in his eyes. 'Babies have to be ... er ... procreated.'

She knew he was referring to that moment of withdrawal, and his subsequent promise to give her time.

'I do know the facts of life,' she said calmly. 'I'm sure everything will be all right once we're married.'

Surely then the shadow of Panos would be removed for ever.

Cass arranged that he would take her into Corfu next day, when she could change her cheques and buy more clothes and other necessities, including a suitcase, and he would enquire about their flight. He hoped to be able to book one within the next few days. She need not fear to be seen now she was his fiancée. If anyone was enquiring for Simonides' missing secretary, he would admit to having rescued her from the sea, but she was under his protection now.

They set off next day in Cass's car, driving along a rutted track which eventually reached a tarmac road. Rachel had an odd sensation of having been away from civilisation for a long period. So much had happened during her brief stay at Aghios Petros. She had been near to death, recovered and become engaged to be married. Seated beside Cass as the car rattled through olive groves and vineyards, she thought it was impossible that he had only just come into her life, but he was not an utter stranger. She had known his name, read articles he had written and one of his books before she met him. Angus had admired his work. Angus. How she wished her father was still alive! He would have been thrilled to learn that she was to marry Caspar Dakers, and she was sure that the two men would have been compatible. She had told Cass she hoped to come to love him; was she already moving in that direction? Could one fall in love in so short a time? She glanced at the lean brown profile beside her, watched his capable hands manipulating the steering wheel. She was uncertain about the state of her feelings, but she did know that if he went out of her life now he would leave an enormous gap.

When they reached their destination, Rachel looked anxiously towards the sea, but there was no luxury yacht at anchor in the harbour, only a cruise liner disgorging passengers. Cass found a parking place near the centre of the town so it would be handy for their parcels.

Since Rachel had not been in Corfu Town before, Cass showed her the sights, the two Venetian forts, seen from the mountain side, called the old and the new, Saint Spyridon's church and the long arcade of the Liston Mansion looking on to the open square, with trees, green spaces and the cricket pitch. They wandered along the narrow alleyways filled with shops and Rachel made her purchases, including a cotton frock and some more underwear, a suitcase and a handbag. Cass bought her a ring, a half hoop of brilliants. She had been taken with an opal one, liking the milky stones, but he had objected. Opals were unlucky, and though she had declared she was not superstitious, he had insisted, for in their peculiar circumstances they could not afford to risk their luck.

They drank coffee sitting out in the open and then Cass in fun bought for her an enormous straw hat from a tourist souvenir shop. She had braided her plaits round her head, but to accommodate the hat, she let them fall.

'Now you look like a milkmaid,' he told her.

'More like a mushroom. I think I'll have my hair cut off.'

'That you won't, not while you're contracted to me. That's why I'm marrying you.'

'To gain possession of my hair? I could give you the severed plaits.'

'I'd prefer them attached to your head. Seriously, Rachel, I'd hate you to cut off your hair.'

As he had assumed proprietorial rights, Rachel supposed he was entitled to some say in her appearance. She promised she would retain her flowing locks.

As they strolled along she noticed how often strangers glanced curiously at her companion, especially women. With his slanted eyes and carved features he did not look Greek or Italian and certainly not Anglo-Saxon. Neither had he the flat face of the Slav. She could imagine him superbly mounted galloping across the immense Hungarian plain as his mother's ancestors must have done inspecting some vast estate, and exercising the *droit de seigneur*. For he could be no peasant's son; the haughty curve of his nostrils, the proud carriage of his head spoke of race. However casually he was clad, Cass would always appear distinguished, and even the unobservant tourists noticed his quality.

Today he was in a carefree mood and they laughed
and teased each other over their shopping as if there
had never been any dark undercurrents in their relationship. The sun shone upon white buildings and red
roofs, and Rachel was happy, even gay. They reached a
junction where roads went in several directions, with
the end of Liston Arcade on their right, and the façade
of the Governor's palace nearly in front of them. They
halted under a palm tree, watching a carriage go past
drawn by a bonneted horse, the driver sitting on the
box and an awning fixed over the old-fashioned back
seats. Such vehicles were for hire in the town.

'Would you like a drive in one of those?' Cass asked
Rachel, but she did not answer. She was frozen into
petrified immobility as she caught sight of the woman
who had come round the corner from the arcade.
Dressed in white with a pink parasol held affectedly
over one shoulder, she was perfectly groomed from the
fair hair glimpsed under her little white hat to her high-
heeled kid shoes. She even wore gloves. She was not
young, but every art had been used to preserve the
illusion of youth. She was beautiful and she had style.

'What is it?' Cass asked. Then he too saw the lady.
'Good God!' he exclaimed, and paled under his tan.
'It can't be!'

He grabbed Rachel's arm and turned as if to flee,
but they were hemmed in by pedestrians and traffic.
The woman had seen them, she closed her parasol and
quickened her pace, a patter of her heels on the pave-
ment, her large blue eyes expressed delight.

'My darling child! So you're safe, thank God!'

At the sound of her voice, Cass grew rigid, and
Rachel answered.

'Yes, Mother, I survived,' she said drily, staring

stonily at the enchanting vision in front of her. 'Thanks to this gentleman. This is my mother, Cass, Desirée Lorraine. Mother, meet Caspar Dakers.'

Desirée's blue gaze moved to Cass. 'Is it really you?' she exclaimed. 'But of course, you've a villa on Corfu. We don't need an introduction, Ray, we're very old friends.' She held out her gloved hand. 'How are you, Cass? What a coincidence meeting you with my daughter!'

Glancing swiftly at the man beside her, Rachel saw his face had become as set and hard as marble. He barely touched Desirée's outstretched fingers. She surmised that they had met in the television studios, but though the possibility had occurred to her before, she had decided the acquaintanceship could only have been transitory and neither had ever mentioned the other. Now, from Cass's strained expression and Desirée's coquettish air together with her claim that he was an old friend, it occurred to her that they had been something more than friends. The thought turned her cold. Cass and Desirée—the combination was repugnant to her.

'I thought you'd gone on to Athens,' she said coldly.

'How could I until I discovered what had happened to you?' The blue eyes were full of reproach. 'Panos had to go, his business couldn't wait, but I stayed hoping for news of you. We were both frantic when we reached Corfu and you couldn't be found. Nobody had seen you, you'd just vanished.' She waved her hand dramatically. 'Where did you get to?'

'I ... fell into the sea,' Rachel told her without expression.

'You mean you went overboard? But how could you? Didn't anyone see you ... hear you?'

'Apparently not.'

In every nerve Rachel was conscious of Cass still and silent beside her. What was he thinking? She had told him she was alone in the world, and here was an apparently loving mother anxious to claim her. An obviously affluent woman who was an old friend of his.

'Panos said you'd had a tiff,' Desirée went on in her clear light voice. 'So foolish of you, darling, to quarrel with him, but it's part of being in love, I know.' She laughed a musical tinkle of sound. 'But wasn't to go overboard rather extreme? You might have been drowned.'

'I was, very nearly.'

Desirée gave her a sharp look in which was no affection. Rachel could believe in her anxiety, Desirée feared she had lost the key that was to unlock Simonides' treasure chests, but she had no real love for her daughter. This display of maternal solicitude was an act, put on for Cass's benefit. The actress turned to Cass with a charming shrug of her shoulders.

'These young lovers, always so intense. Panos is engaged to my daughter, Cass. Such a wonderful match for her. He'll be so delighted and thankful to know she's safe.' She turned back to Rachel. 'You naughty girl! You should have let us know at once where you were. Had you no thought for our anguish? Poor Panos, I must send a radiogram immediately.'

'You'll do no such thing,' Rachel said fiercely, a recurrence of her old terror sweeping over her. She turned desperately to Cass. 'I'm not engaged to Panos Simonides. Young lovers indeed! He's an old satyr.'

'Be quiet!' Desirée glanced at the passers-by as if she feared someone would overhear and report to the Greek. 'Of course you're engaged to Panos. It was understood when we went aboard the *Nausicaa*. You can't back out now.' Her voice became shrill with suppressed fury. 'Don't be such a little idiot, Ray! Surely you can make up your differences, knowing how much is at stake?'

Now people were glancing at them curiously, for they made a strange group, the silent distinguished-looking man, the beautiful scolding woman and the girl dressed like a tourist eclipsed by the brim of the large fun hat.

Cass noticed they were attracting attention and intervened.

'It's nearly lunch time. Suppose we go somewhere and eat? Then we can discuss the situation in privacy.'

His voice was cold and clipped. Rachel had no idea of how he was taking her mother's revelations. He had not looked at her throughout the conversation, his eyes being fixed upon Desirée with an unreadable expression. She had an unhappy intuition that he was not thinking about her at all; all his attention was focussed upon her mother. Desirée as usual was exuding charm and elegance, while she, in her trousers and shirt, their pristine freshness soiled by the expedition of the day before, must be looking a tramp.

'A good idea,' Desirée exclaimed. 'Perhaps you can help me, Cass, to persuade this silly little girl of mine where her best interests lie.' She turned to Rachel. 'And take off that idiotic hat! You look like a beachcomber.'

Rachel's response to this command was to jam the offending head gear more firmly on her head. She caught an approving gleam in Cass's eye, and her heart lightened; even though she had misrepresented her circumstances to him, he was not going to desert her, when she needed his help more than ever before. But it sank again and her confidence faded, as Desirée took his arm in a possessive manner and smiled beguilingly up into his face. She stood no chance against her mother's blandishments, and Cass would act as she demanded.

Her heart swelled as conviction grew that Desirée was the woman with the silver-gilt hair who had treated him badly, but whom he never could forget. Rachel had inherited the hair and Desirée's clear-cut features, only her eyes were similar to her father's. So now she knew of whom she had reminded him. He must be considerably younger than Desirée, but he had been old enough to give her a young man's first devotion, which the actress would lap up greedily and have no scruples about discarding him when he became tedious. Surreptitiously, as she followed them, Rachel slipped off her ring and put it into her newly purchased handbag. Proudly she told herself that she did not want her mother's leavings, and the whole situation nauseated her. She glanced round, meditating plunging into the crowd to escape the couple ahead of her, but she could do nothing without her passport and that had been left in Cass's bungalow. Nor was she a coward to shirk the battle ahead of her. She must convince Cass and her mother that she would never consent to be Panos's bride, and here with people all around she would not be helpless as she had been on his yacht.

Cass took them into a restaurant in the Liston building, and found a more or less secluded table. Desirée's manner towards him was blatantly flirtatious. She implied that nothing could be more delightful than to have encountered an old flame who she was sure still admired her. Their first meeting had been in a television canteen when they were both working on different series, but that was before Cass had become rich and famous. It must have been, Rachel calculated, soon after her parents had been divorced and before Desirée's next marriage. Ironically Cass might have become her stepfather, except at that time he was too poor and unknown to be considered eligible as a husband.

At first they were too absorbed in their reminiscences to pay any attention to her. Rachel sat sunk in silent misery, conserving her strength to combat her mother. She had already risked being drowned to escape the fate Desirée planned for her. Cass had offered her protection, and if that were withdrawn she did not know where she could find a refuge. His unrevealing face gave no hint of his reactions, and his head was inclined towards Desirée politely as he listened to her flow of chatter.

Rachel made a mere pretence of eating the food set before her, but her companions did not notice her lack of appetite. Then, when the coffee was served, Desirée opened fire.

'I've done my best for Rachel,' she said plaintively to Cass. 'Given her an excellent education, sent her to a Swiss finishing school to fit her for the highest social position at a cost I couldn't really afford. All I ask in return is that she should make a good marriage. She hasn't any particular talents and though you wouldn't think it seeing her now,' she threw a disparaging glance at her daughter, her face obscured by the straw hat, 'her looks are an asset, about her only one.'

'She's inherited them from her mother,' Cass said gallantly.

Desirée smiled complacently. 'Of course, she's not

like her father. He was a worthy man, but so dull.'

Rachel sat up, straightening herself in her chair, a bright spot of colour on either cheek.

'I didn't find him so. I loved him.' Her voice shook. She controlled it, and went on: 'Would you mind not talking about me as if I wasn't here?'

'So you've found your tongue at last,' Desirée observed scathingly. 'Now please, miss, may we have an explanation of your extraordinary conduct?'

'I should have thought it was obvious. I'd rather drown than marry Panos Simonides.'

Desirée threw her eyes towards the ceiling. 'Such perversity!' she sighed. She turned to Cass. 'I don't know what got into her. For a man like Panos who could have any woman he wanted, the offer of his hand was a great honour. What's more, she accepted him.' She flashed round on Rachel. 'You can't play fast and loose with a man like Panos!'

Rachel sighed. She saw Cass was looking at her with astonishment. Of course he would agree with her mother. Panos, incredibly rich and influential, was a catch any girl would be jubilant to have made. That the man filled her with aversion did not matter. Women could endure worse things for the sake of wealth and position. She had not told Cass that Simonides wanted to marry her; she had implied something else. Cass would see Panos's fiancée and Desirée's daughter in a very different light from the naïve, penniless secretary who had landed herself in a trap. Nor could she now explain, with Desirée present, that she had never really consented to accept Panos's suit. Her mother would contradict every word she uttered and try to make out that she was merely being difficult out of caprice.

When Panos had invited them for a cruise, she had

thought it was Desirée in whom he was interested and her mother wanted her to go along to become acquainted with her future stepfather. She had met the Greek during the year after she left school and had come to live with Desirée. During that time her glamorous idol had begun to topple from its pedestal. At close quarters she could not fail to notice Desirée Lorraine's selfishness and avarice. As she rarely obtained engagements nowadays, Desirée was looking for a source of income.

Once on board, Rachel discovered her mistake. Panos began to woo her in a heavy-handed, possessive way that terrified her. One night after dinner, finding her alone upon the deck, he had become amorous. The great bull of a man with his coarse laugh was utterly repugnant to her. She had torn herself from his arms and fled to her mother's cabin for safety. Desirée had told her not to be a fool, she must accept Panos; such a chance would never come her way again. Filled with horror, Rachel had declared she would rather die, and Desirée had slapped her face and told her not to be hysterical.

Then she changed to appeal. Rachel did not realise how much she had spent upon her for just such an end. She was heavily in debt and Panos had promised to pay whatever she owed as soon as Rachel became his wife. The young girl's reluctance had fired him with a lust for conquest.

Rachel, although shaken, remained obdurate, and then her mother told her that Panos was sailing for Athens where their engagement would be announced. If Rachel continued unco-operative, she would be confined on one of the remote islands that he owned until she came to her senses—and, Desirée added with a significant smile, he would visit her there to add to his persuasions.

'Which you may find a little rough,' she concluded. 'Better take him before you have to.'

Whether this programme was correct or an invention of Desirée's to frighten her daughter into acquiescence, Rachel did not stay to query. She made her few preparations and dived into the sea. She carried away with her the knowledge that the mother she had once loved and revered had betrayed her and become her worst enemy.

Looking now at the beautiful flawless face in which the blue eyes were hard as stones, Rachel declared forcibly:

'I'm not playing fast and loose with anybody. I never said I'd marry him, and I won't.'

Desirée gave an exasperated sigh, and Cass, rather to Rachel's surprise, came to her assistance.

'You mustn't be too hard on Rachel,' he said gently. 'The poor girl was washed ashore at Aghios Petros, a remote hamlet in the north-east. She was suffering from shock and had lost her memory. Fortunately I was at home and was able to help her. It was only today that she remembered who she was and where she came from.'

'Then perhaps she'll also remember her duty in due course,' Desirée snapped. Neither face nor voice expressed the slightest concern for her daughter's plight. Since Rachel had turned up, apparently unharmed, her mind was set upon returning her to Panos Simonides before the Greek changed his mind. He would not be flattered to know that Rachel had preferred a watery death to marrying him.

A look passed between Cass and Rachel and she gave

him a tremulous smile of gratitude. He had trotted out
the story he had prepared for inquisitive officials to
shield her. Perhaps he was going to take her part
against Desirée after all. She raised her left hand to
straighten her hat brim and exposed the absence of his
ring. Instantly his expression changed to sardonic
amusement and he said suavely :

'I can't imagine any daughter of yours, Desirée, passing up a chance of great wealth. Perhaps she thought
Simonides was cooling off and staged this little charade
to increase his desire. Men can lose interest in a too
willing captive. I'm sure you'll be able to persuade
her to go back to him.'

Each biting word fell like a flail upon Rachel's sensitive nerves. Her face whitened and her hand dropped
to her knee. She had hoped for an ally, but he had
joined the enemy. She looked down at her ringless hand
and only then realised what she had done. By taking
off his ring in that moment of foolish pique she had
alienated him. He thought her action indicated that she
had thrown him over for the man she detested. How
could she have been so incredibly idiotic! She should
have flaunted that ring before her mother's eyes and
boldly declared that she had found another man. The
discovery that Cass had been involved with Desirée had
thrown her temporarily, and now it was too late to make
her announcement. She sensed that the revelation of
her parentage had come to Cass as an unwelcome surprise. He must know that Desirée was mercenary and
unscrupulous and what she had done to him had made
him a cynic. Now Rachel's behaviour was convincing
him that she was another of the same breed, that her
precipitate flight had been a stunt to increase Panos's
ardour, that she was deceitful and capricious, and had

never intended to take his proposal seriously.

Desirée had noticed her agitation and a new thought occurred to her.

'Aghios Petros,' she murmured reflectively. 'That's where you live, isn't it, Cass? So Rachel has been with you during this period of ... er ... amnesia.'

'I was privileged to assist her,' he returned coolly. 'And of course as soon as she recovered her memory I brought her here to try and get in touch with you.'

Desirée looked at him suspiciously.

'You didn't seem to be trying very hard when I met you,' she observed. 'In fact you were quite astonished to see me.' She leaned back in her chair smiling mischievously. 'Rachel also wouldn't be a child of mine if she didn't try to make the running with an attractive man. I don't grudge you a bit of fun, my dears, so long as you understand it's over now. Rachel, do be careful what you say to Panos. Greeks are very particular about their wives' conduct, and he believes you're an innocent virgin.'

Snatching up her handbag, Rachel sprang to her feet with a choking sensation. 'I'm going,' she cried. 'I can't stand any more of your taunts!'

'Ray, stop!' Desirée put a gloved hand upon her arm, but Rachel brushed it off and pushed past her. She walked blindly through the restaurant, intent only upon escaping from her tormentors. She traversed the length of the colonnade in its cool shade, then when she reached the end and the glare of the sunlight hit her, she stopped, uncertain which way to go. Where could she go? Desirée would contact Simonides and he would come back to retrieve her, but she no longer felt her old terror of him, for her mind was focussed upon Cass. How happy they had been that morning, until they had run into Desirée and all their plans had been shattered. She had ceased to be repelled by the connection between Cass and her mother, it had happened a long time ago, and did not excuse her idiocy in discarding Cass's ring, but she was uneasily aware that he was falling again under the older woman's spell. Desirée could exert an irresistible charm when she chose, and throughout their lunch she had been favouring him with sidelong glances and inviting looks, even while she was scolding her daughter. 'A lover once will always love again.' Where had she read that? Influenced by Desirée, she could no longer count upon Cass to befriend her, and she was assailed by an unbearable feeling of loss. He had been her one friend in an inimical world and now he had returned to his old allegiance to side against her.

A wave of nausea swept over her and she leaned against the stone arch of the arcade, closing her eyes, her hat tipped over her face. Several of the passing people looked at her, shrugged their shoulders and went on. They decided she was some hippy type overcome by drink or drugs and best avoided.

A hand descending like a steel clamp upon her shoulder caused Rachel to start violently.

'So you didn't get far,' said Cass. 'We spotted you as soon as we came out of the restaurant and you conveniently stayed put while we decided what to do with you.'

Rachel's eyes flew open, and she pushed back her hat, to see with relief that he was alone.

'Where's Mother?'

'Gone back to her hotel to recover from the stress of our meeting,' he told her drily. 'I'm to take you back to Aghios Petros.'

Hope flared up in her. 'To ... stay?'

'Not on your life! Now that I know you have a living parent I can thankfully surrender my responsibility in the right quarter. Miss Lorriane,' his voice rasped on the name, 'will come to collect you.'

Keeping his hand upon her shoulder, he propelled her towards the spot where his car was parked.

'Cass,' she began desperately, 'it wasn't like she said. Let me tell you everything, I'd like to, but don't turn against me. You're the only person I can trust.'

'You haven't trusted me,' Cass pointed out. 'You described your situation entirely inaccurately. Like your mother, you're devious and cunning. No doubt you derived a good deal of secret amusement from my efforts on your behalf, but I don't enjoy being made a fool of by a chit like you.'

Rachel wilted under his contempt. Desirée had been working upon him to represent her in the worst possible light, and she did not know what she could say to soften him.

They had reached the car, and unlocking the door he bundled her unceremoniously into the passenger seat. In spite of his uncompromising attitude Rachel had not entirely given up hope.

Once in the peace and quiet of the bungalow, away from Desirée's pervasive influence, she would make him listen to her, point out that what she had told him had only differed from actuality in a few unimportant details. So, as he took his place beside her, her optimism rose. But she had forgotten two things; firstly that her close physical resemblance to Desirée who had injured him would make whatever she said suspect, and that she had discarded his ring.

As the car sped away from the town she drew a long breath of relief.

'Oh, I'll be glad to get home!'

'It isn't your home,' he corrected her harshly. 'When you've sorted out your belongings and packed them in that new suitcase and collected your passport, Desirée will come for you this evening. She'll expect to find you properly dressed and without that hat.'

He took a hand from the wheel and whisked off the offending headgear from her head, throwing it on to the back seat.

It seemed to Rachel that with it went the carefree mood of the morning and all the happy hours they had spent together. Until that moment she had not known how happy they had been. A sob rose in her throat and Cass said brutally:

'You needn't turn on the waterworks, they won't move me. You're your mother's child, Rachel Reed, and I got her measure years ago. I'm sorry for Panos Simonides between the pair of you.'

Rachel turned her head to the window and they completed the journey in silence.

CHAPTER SEVEN

ARRIVED at the bungalow, Cass told Rachel curtly to go inside and he would bring in her parcels. She went disconsolately into the living room which had become so dear and familiar, and stood at the long window staring vacantly at the view of the sea. In less than a week her life had changed and changed again since she had embarked on the yacht at Venice to cruise down the Adriatic. That had culminated in her desperate bid to be rid of Panos and led to her stay with Cass that had brought such high hopes and now their complete reversal. In that short space of time she had met a man who had become the centre of her universe. It was only now, faced with parting, that it came to her that she was on the verge of falling head over heels in love with the cynical author. She had had no time in which her feelings could develop naturally. The swift course of events had ripened the fruit before it had even formed from the opening bud of incipient passion. If they had not met Desirée, if Cass had carried out his plan of taking her to England for their marriage, it would have bloomed and expanded in the sunshine of his presence, but its forced growth was doomed to wither and die before she was even aware of its potential. She had the feeling that something beautiful had been within her grasp and now it had slipped away.

For during Cass's stony silence on the drive up from Corfu, she had had to realise that he was hopelessly estranged. His proposal had been prompted by a chivalrous impulse to protect a friendless girl fleeing from an amorous satyr. That the girl attracted him physically had been some compensation for the loss of his freedom, but he had never given the slightest indication that he loved her or could ever come to love her.

He had said carelessly that the chances of their marriage working out were about equal to those of most couples embarking upon this hazardous undertaking—not the words of a lover who believed blindly that the union must endure by reason of the strength of his passion. He would consider that the morning's revelations had released him from his bond and abandon her without regret. For the case against her was black. He had learned that she had lied to him about her position, that she was not a working girl deluded by Panos's promises to take an ambiguous situation as his employee, but a socialite, trained to sell herself to the highest bidder. That she had gone aboard the *Nausicaa* at the invitation of its owner, who was her declared suitor, under her mother's wing. None of this she could deny. She could never hope to convince him that Panos had threatened her, and upon calm reflection she had come to doubt that he had. It was her unscrupulous mother who had invented the story about being incarcerated upon an inaccessible island, and her repulsion for the man and fear had caused her to believe it.

Added to this, that same mother had turned out to be the old flame of Cass's to whom he attributed the loss of his young illusions and the basest motives for all her actions. Vaguely she was aware that because of their physical likeness he was identifying her with Desirée, and as a result had become incensed against her, believing she had deliberately played upon his good nature for her amusement, while marking time to consider her next move.

By stripping off his ring, he took it, she had indicated that she had no intention of admitting to Desirée or Panos that she had become engaged to him. Rachel suspected that he was secretly a little ashamed of the impulse that had prompted his proposal. Chivalry was a dead word in the era of Women's Lib, and not what was expected of a tough guy, which was what Caspar Dakers was reputed to be, so that any appeal to him for clemency and understanding was unlikely to make any impression. If he intended to flay her with his scorn and derision it was no more than he believed she deserved.

Nevertheless she was determined to try to make him listen to her, and persuade him that she had some excuse for her actions. He could not be so unjust as to dismiss her without a hearing.

She looked round the room which at first sight had seemed so plain and austere. Desirée had always filled her various flats with much greater luxury, and the Swiss school had been expensively furished, but the simplicity of Cass Dakers's abode had appealed to Rachel, who disliked ornate embellishments. She realised with a sense of shock that the days she had spent here were among the happiest of her life, and she would have asked for nothing better than to have lived here . . . with Cass.

She heard his footsteps cross the hall and the thud as he dropped her parcels on the floor. She had bought a green linen dress which he had said would suit her, and had meant to put it on this evening to please him. She would not be here that night.

She sensed his presence behind her, though she had not heard him enter the room; the matting deadened his approach. Slowly she turned round to face him and for a few moments they stared at each other in silence. Rachel's green-clad figure looked pathetically young and defenceless, her plaits making her appear still a schoolgirl. Her big eyes were full of the wistful appeal that her lips were too proud to utter. Against his will, the man's hard face softened and he passed his hand wearily across his brow.

'You've inherited not only her looks but your mother's talent for acting,' he said almost gently. 'You appear the picture of wronged innocence.' He sighed. 'She could look like that too, when she wanted to get her own way.'

'How well did you know her?' Rachel asked curiously. Cass must have met her mother at a time when she herself had been a young child.

He smiled wryly. 'Not at all, as it turned out. We met in the studio canteen; she'd been rehearsing and was dressed much as you are now, and she looked about eighteen, though she must have been a good deal older. I imagined she was about my own age, but boys haven't a clue about a woman's age, though I soon realised she couldn't be so young to have got where she had. I lost my youthful heart to her there and then, but of course I had nothing to offer her. I was only at the beginning of things. Actually I was there that day to earn a few additional pence as an extra.' He was gazing past Rachel to the sunlit terrace beyond the window, his thoughts re-creating the distant past. His face wore a sad, dreamy look that was quite out of his normal character, and he appeared much younger, the youth he once had been. Rachel was conscious of a

dull ache in the region of her heart which she recognised
with surprise as jealousy. Cass had loved her mother;
perhaps she had been the only woman he truly had.

'She pretended my poverty didn't matter,' Cass went
on. 'She declared that ours was a great love, she even
said she'd marry me when she was free. Actually she
was already divorced, but I didn't know that, nor did
she reveal her real name. Of course she was only
amusing herself with me, my devotion flattered her, and
she could play me off against the rich fellow she did
eventually marry. But fool that I was . . . I believed
her.'

He fell silent, still wrapped in the past, with the unfamiliar almost boyish look upon his face. Rachel was
submerged in a turmoil of mixed emotions. Pity for his
past pain, anger against her mother, the jealousy which
she could not subdue, and a wild regret that it was
Desirée whom he had loved and that she herself could
not reach him.

Cass brought his gaze back from the window and
recollected time and place. His expression changed to
one of wry humour. He was Caspar Dakers again, the
worldly cynic.

'That's all over, thank God,' he said fervently. 'I
hadn't thought of her for years until I met you. Sit
down, girl, and wipe that look off your face, you're
making me feel maudlin.'

He walked over to a cupboard in the corner where
he kept his drinks and poured himself a stiff whisky
and soda.

'Would you like a drink?' he asked perfunctorily.

Rachel shook her head. She sat down in one of the
armchairs, crossing her long legs.

'You're prejudiced against me because I favour

Mother in looks,' she accused him, opening her case for the defence. 'That's hardly fair, because my *character* is quite different.'

He raised his brows in disbelief. At that moment the foreign element in him was very marked, his normal casual good humour replaced by a venom that sharpened both his features and his voice. His eyes appeared narrower, his brows more slanted, and bitter lines were drawn about his mouth. Rachel feared that his incursion into the past had revived his resentment against Desirée and he was about to assuage the wounds inflicted upon his ego in her absence by venting his animosity upon herself. Vaguely she wondered if Hungarians were a vindictive people; she did not know, but she surmised they were proud. This half-bred scion of the Magyar race looked capable of any outrage if he were offended.

'You surprise me,' he sneered. 'It seems to me you're running true to Desirée's form and playing the same game—two men on one string. If you were really honest, you'd have told your mother you were engaged to me instead of hiding your ring. That would have scotched her plans, but oh no ... you were having second thoughts about ditching Simonides. I'm reputed to be wealthy, but this poor little place hardly bears that out. Perhaps you wanted to check my bank balance before you committed yourself.'

Rachel's eyes flashed. 'How dare you make such a suggestion!' she blazed. 'You're insufferable!'

'How dare you try to play with me? When I so unwisely leaped into the breach, you hadn't told me Simonides wanted to marry you. That makes rather a difference.'

'No difference at all—I loathe the man. What did make a difference was the discovery that you'd been my mother's lover. It ... it's almost indecent!'

Cass refilled his glass. His pale eyes were glittering between his narrowed lids. Rachel had the horrific impression that he was actually enjoying insulting her. All the accumulated bitterness of years had overflowed and was being poured upon her innocent head.

'I was never her lover technically,' he told her. 'That's what counts. It was all cobwebs and moonshine ... what fools the young can be! But I'm forgetting, you're young too, but I'm sure you'd never be so foolish as to throw away the substance for the shadow, however attractively it's parcelled. Under that innocent façade of yours there dwells a scheming little mind, and you weren't sure if my financial status was solid enough to justify losing Simonides.'

Rachel had gone very white under this attack, but she responded with spirit. He was reacting far worse than she had ever anticipated, but she refused to be cowed.

'How you do harp upon money,' she said disdainfully. 'It really doesn't mean anything to me. But I did have second thoughts about our engagement.' He gave an exclamation of triumph and she looked at him reproachfully. 'Not for any of your reasons but because I felt I was using you as a means of escape. It wasn't fair to you.' She looked away towards the window. Actually this argument had only just occurred to her, but she ought to have thought of it before. She said very low, 'It wasn't as though you ... I ... we loved each other.'

There was a short silence, while Cass gazed at her averted face with a curious expression. Then he laughed. Draining his glass, he set it down so violently on the table that it cracked.

'Don't for God's sake dish me up any of that romantic twaddle,' he said roughly. 'Your concern for me would be touching if it were genuine, but you've only just thought that one up.' Rachel flushed, for that was true, he was much too discerning. He went on relentlessly. 'You've your mother's gift for putting an artful gloss upon the most treacherous actions.'

Rachel stood up and walked across to him. She saw his movement of withdrawal as she approached and his action stabbed her. She said composedly:

'Will you please try to get it into your thick head that Mother and I are two different people. All those abominable things you've been saying are directed against her, not me. I'm the same Rachel who cooked for you, climbed Pantokrator with you, and ... and ...' her voice trembled but she quickly controlled it, 'shopped with you in Corfu this morning. You didn't dislike and despise me then, did you?'

His eyes dropped before her steady gaze and he moved uncomfortably.

'I didn't know then who you were,' he mumbled.

'And now you do, you can't forgive me for being my mother's daughter? I didn't choose her. I much preferred my father. He was genuine right through, but I didn't find her out until recently.'

A spasm crossed her face; she too had had her disillusionment where Desirée was concerned. 'She's so beautiful, so glamorous,' she murmured. 'I thought she was an angel when I was a child.'

'Because angels are usually depicted with blue eyes and golden hair,' he said drily. He lifted his head and they stared at each other. They were so near that they were almost touching and Rachel was glad that she had not inherited Desirée's blue orbs, and her own hazel ones could not remind him of her, for doubtless in those far off days of their love he had gazed as intently into their blue depths as he was doing now into hers.

'What colour are your eyes?' he asked. 'Grey, green, amber, they change with the light. Definitely not angel's eyes.' His voice thickened. 'You're beautiful too, Rachel, a sea witch to steal men's souls.'

'I don't care for the fancy stuff,' Rachel remarked, suppressing her rising elation. 'I've no designs upon your soul, which I'm sure you don't believe you've got. I only want your good opinion.'

She misread his expression, which had she been more sophisticated she would have known indicated that his thoughts were definitely not upon angels. Believing he was softening, she acted unwisely. She raised her arms and clasped his neck, murmuring softly, 'Cass, Cass, you can't really think so badly of me.'

His reaction was what she should have anticipated, a swift and violent embrace, so cruel that she felt her bones must crack. His mouth came down on hers with fierce intensity, her slim pliant body was moulded against his muscular strength and her senses reeled under his savage onslaught.

But his spurt of passion died as quickly as it had erupted. And he flung her away from him so hard that she lost her balance and falling against the arm of a chair, collapsed on the floor beside it.

'Never touch me again, you little tart, or I'll strangle you with your own hair!' he snarled.

Rachel received this charming remark in shocked silence. He had interpreted her gesture of affectionate appeal as deliberate provocation. There had been no tenderness in that cruel embrace, he had only been venting his past frustrations. She had suffered the final humiliation and her heart was as hot and sore as her bruised lips. She felt that she hated Caspar Dakers.

Cass glanced uneasily at her huddled form with compunction. She looked like a broken flower, so still and pale, one unravelled plait covering her like a silken web of silvery gold. He cleared his throat and asked anxiously :

'Are you hurt?'

She lifted her head, parting her hair with trembling fingers and gazed at him with sad reproach.

'Not physically.'

Cass turned away, the set of his shoulders registering faint shame, but it was not in his nature to apologise for what he considered was her just deserts.

'I always said you were a menace,' he excused himself. 'A disturber of the peace.'

'Well, I'll soon be gone,' she reminded him. 'Then you can enjoy your solitude again.'

He seemed about to make some protest, but checked himself. Much of his former harshness had evaporated, the lines had disappeared from around his mouth, and his eyes held their familiar mocking glint.

'If you're all right, get up,' he bade her not unkindly. 'You look far too humble crouched at my feet, and you're not humble, are you, Rachel? Would you like a drink to restore you?'

'No, thank you.' She struggled to her feet, noticing he made no movement to help her. Did he consider her touch contaminating?

'I dislike you, Caspar Dakers,' she said deliberately.

For a moment he looked startled, then he laughed.

'The eternal feminine caprice, now hot, now cold, but I'm afraid you'll be gone before the warm spell

sets in again ... no, don't rend me,' as she opened her
mouth, 'there isn't time for a sparring match.' He
glanced at his watch. 'You must get ready to receive
your mother.' His manner changed to brisk command.
'You bought a dress this morning, you'd better go and
put it on. And pack the rest of your gear. Be sure you
don't leave anything behind.' He smiled wryly. 'We
don't want any incriminating evidence brought to light.
You have been occupying my bedroom.'

So she had deprived him of it, though he had made
light of it, saying he used the divan in his work room
whenever he had a guest. She had accepted his statement without query, but now it seemed rather inadequate. She said haltingly:

'It was very good of you to turn out for me. I hope
you haven't been very uncomfortable.'

'Not as regards sleeping quarters,' he said significantly. 'But do run along and make yourself presentable. You look as though you'd been pulled through a
hedge backwards.'

Rachel began to plait her loosened hair.

'Whose fault was that?'

'That's debatable, but you don't want your mother
to suspect what happened.'

She flushed. 'No, of course not, but I'm not going to
change. She'll have to put up with my slacks and top.'

She could not bear to put on the linen dress that had
been chosen for Cass. Let his last sight of her be how
he had always seen her, an urchin in casual wear.

'Desirée won't like it,' he warned her. 'In spite of
her peculiar morals, your mother is a stickler for ap-
pearances. She wants you to arrive at her hotel respect-
ably clad and with luggage.'

Rachel winced, recalling Desirée's immaculate garb.

She had had more than one tussle with her over clothes. She had wanted to overdress her like an expensive doll.

'These,' she touched her trousers, 'are perfectly respectable, and only two days old. All the girls wear them. Incidentally, couldn't you have brought my things to Corfu without dragging me back here to collect them?'

She had been too absorbed with Cass and his reactions to question that before. Perhaps she had even been cherishing a hope that he wanted to give her a chance to explain herself, but that, as it transpired, had not been his purpose.

'Because you had to be here to support the story she's going to tell Simonides. According to her you were found on the beach here in a state of collapse, and have been ill ever since. Mine being the only civilised habitation within miles, you were brought here and my housekeeper nursed you—no need to mention that I haven't got one. Simonides would find that quite incredible, no one in his world would so much as boil an egg if they could pay someone else to do it for them. There was some delay in tracing your mother, but as soon as she was advised of your whereabouts, she radioed Simonides, which she will have done by now, and arranged to hire a car to come and fetch you. She did suggest applying for an ambulance, but I thought that was overdoing it. This morning, of course, never happened. All you have to do is to play the convalescent invalid. I suggest a thick application of white powder and some eye-shadow before you meet your intended.'

'He's not my intended,' Rachel reiterated with exasperation. It seemed all her denials had made no impression upon Cass at all. Or perhaps he believed what he wanted to believe. It suited him to insist that she was going to be reconciled with the Greek because it freed him from any further responsibility towards her. Desirée's ingenious twisting of the facts filled her with repugnance. She must be quick-witted to have thought of all that during the short period they had been watching her in the arcade, but Rachel had no intention of playing the part assigned to her.

'I'm not going to support that false tale,' she said firmly. 'I shall tell the truth.'

'You can't do that!' Cass looked alarmed. 'If you spread it around that you spent three days alone here with me, you know what will be said.'

'It won't be true, and I can't help it if people have nasty minds. You blame me for not being straight with you, but I didn't inform you of the real facts because I couldn't bring myself to confess to a stranger that my own mother had engineered such an impossible situation. But I've learnt my lesson. There'll be no more lies.'

'I applaud your belated honesty,' Cass said sarcastically. 'You might have had qualms at the beginning, but I think I deserved to know the truth when I asked you to marry me. However, that's beside the point now, as I'm not going to marry you.' Rachel flinched at this calm assertion. 'But you'll do yourself no good by making yourself a target for mud-slinging. Much better let your mother handle the situation. She'd get away with murder.'

Rachel's lips set mutinously. She needed a little time to decide what she was going to do, but she was not going back to Corfu to be a pawn in her mother's game. Cass looked at her unresponsive face, and scratched his head in perplexity.

'I can't make you out, Rachel,' he exclaimed. 'If you

want to defy your mother, you had the opportunity this morning, but you didn't take it. That reminds me, would you be so good as to return my ring? It was a good one and I don't see why I should make you a present of it, since you spurn the donor.'

'But I don't ...' She broke off, biting her lip. What was the good of offering explanations to Cass when he did not want to accept them? It was more dignified to pretend an indifference that she did not feel.

'I'd no intention of keeping it,' she said haughtily, and picking up her handbag she took out the half-hoop of stones. For a moment she held it between her fingers watching the bright light strike fire from the brilliants. How different Cass had been that morning when he had put it on her finger! How many broken romances had terminated with the return of a ring, with perhaps heartbreak on one side and repudiation on the other. She sighed and handed it to him.

'Thank you for the gesture,' she said quietly. Then with an effort to preserve her pride, 'It was a nice thought, but I'm sure it would never have worked.'

'Perhaps not.' He took it from her. 'You changed your mind very suddenly.'

'How do you suppose I felt when we met Mother and I discovered she was the woman you'd always been in love with?' she demanded, returning to her original cause for affront. 'And whom you're still obsessed with,' she added.

'She doesn't obsess me. I'd forgotten her until you came along with her hair, which always fascinated me.' She thought his denial was a little too emphatic. He threw her a penetrating glance, through narrowed lids. 'Don't tell me you took my ring off out of childish pique?'

'No, of course not!' Rachel was equally emphatic, though she was unhappily aware that her motive had been just that. 'It was seeing you with her made me realise the great gap between us.'

Which was not really true, she had never felt a gap between herself and Cass although he was so much older, not since she had come to know him better, though at first his sophistication had awed her. Cass was studying her quizzically, absently throwing the ring up into the air and catching it.

'You don't know what you do want,' he told her. Then he said very deliberately, for he wanted to shock her into the realisation of what telling the truth might cost her, 'But for heaven's sake be discreet. If you go blurting out the truth, as you call it, you'll find yourself branded as one of my women—a subject for sniggers and prurient curiosity. I shan't mind, nor will the usual run of females who honour me with their favours, they're hard-bitten and know their world. We laugh it off and go our several ways, but you, I fancy, are more sensitive.'

Rachel flushed and paled at this plain speaking. One of Cass Dakers' women ... horrible suggestion, she could not bear that. As for Cass, he was without shame.

'Very well,' she said tonelessly. 'I'll support Mother's story, up to a point.' It would not help her in her quest for work if there was a scandal about her. She told him that.

'No, it wouldn't,' he agreed. He grinned impishly. 'You might even get your picture in the Sunday papers: Young socialite who threw over a millionaire for a liaison with well-known author ...'

'Shut up!' Rachel said fiercely, finding his perverse humour unbearable. 'That isn't funny.'

'Sorry, but seriously, you won't need a job.'

'Oh yes, I shall, I'm not going back to Mother. She can say that bit about me being ill and the housekeeper, but I refuse to be escorted as a wilting invalid back to Corfu.'

Her brows knitted in thought. In a short while Desirée would be arriving and if she were not going with her she would have to find somewhere to go. Hide on the mountain? The mountain. Eileen Stavros ... the woman with the kind blue eyes so different from Desirée's, who told her to come to her if ever she were in trouble. Eileen was a Celt and might have even forseen this very situation. Celts had the Sight. Rachel drew a long breath of relief, recalling the small stone house on the hillside. There she could find refuge until the talk, if there was any, blew over and there she would be safe from both Cass and Simonides, as behind a convent wall.

'You'll have to go,' Cass insisted. 'You can't stay here.'

'I wouldn't want to, even if you begged me to,' she said proudly, and had to make an effort to stop her lips from trembling. If Cass begged her to stay, she would be unable to resist him, but the last thing he wanted was to keep her there. 'For the time being, I shall go to Eileen Stavros.'

'What?'

'She told me I could, if I needed a friend.'

His face expressing lively consternation, Cass declared:

'But my dear girl, that's out of the question. Oh, Eileen's a good sort. She's a weak spot for any sort of stray.' Rachel winced, for was she not a stray or waif? A sea waif cast up by the tide, with no place to go. 'I don't doubt she'll welcome you, but her house is primitive in the extreme. You'll find hens laying in your bed, pigs invading the living room, and there's no mod cons—I think she washes in the rainwater barrel. You can't go there, Rachel.'

'I can and I will. I don't mind a bit of hardship. I was sickened by the luxury on Panos's yacht, the simple life will be a nice change.'

Cass sat down in an armchair staring at her.

'I really believe you mean it!'

'I can't put it any plainer, can I? I'll go and pack up my things and then I'll be off. I'd like to get away before Mother comes, and it's a long way.'

'It is that.' He seemed genuinely concerned. When he spoke again there was a note of feeling in his voice. 'Rachel, I can't let you do this, it's absurd, you're imposing an impossible penance upon yourself.' He stood up and coming across to her, laid a brotherly arm across her shoulders. 'Rachel, I ...'

A quick patter of feet and Dion burst in upon them, his face brilliant with excitement.

'*Kyrie, kyrie*, you back?' he cried, and broke into a flood of Greek.

Cass hastily removed his arm, and moved away from Rachel, who could not understand what Dion was saying. He interpreted for her:

'It seems a motor launch has put into the harbour ... Oh no!'

For Dion had told him who had arrived in it, a name that even to him was familiar. Panos Simonides.

CHAPTER EIGHT

PANOS SIMONIDES was in actual fact not at all the monster Rachel's excited imagination had created. He had been twice married, but neither of his wives had given him the son he desired to inherit his mercantile empire, so he was prepared to make a third attempt. Rachel's youth and aloof air appealed to him, and when Desirée insisted that the girl admired him and was flattered by his attentions, but was too shy to show it, he believed her. Besides, what young girl would not be dazzled by all that he could give her? He did not expect love, but he anticipated that she would be virtuous and faithful.

On board his yacht her modest bearing pleased him and he did not notice the aversion in her eyes or misinterpreted it. No well-bred Greek girl would have been allowed on deck alone, but he knew British manners were freer, and when he came upon Rachel mooning over the rail in solitude, he saw no harm in pressing his suit a little more vigorously than he would have done with one of his own countrywomen. Her violent rebuff did not offend him, he attributed it to bashfulness and a virginal recoil from masculine ardour which he would overcome in due course. Misled by her mother's encouragement as he was, it did not occur to him that she could seriously mean to refuse him. There were far too many women eager to become the third Mrs Simonides and share his fortune for him to give credence to such foolishness.

When the yacht put into Corfu and it was discovered Rachel was not on board, he had had the ship searched from stem to stern and the crew interrogated. The men, to save their own skins, disclaimed all knowledge of her, nor could anyone recollect when she had last been seen. The look-out had noticed something dive into the sea coming through the straits, but knowing there were dolphins there, surmised it was one of those creatures leaping up and falling back into the sea as they frequently did, but he kept that information to himself, fearing instant dismissal if he mentioned it.

Panos had to go on to Athens, but he left Desirée in Corfu to pursue enquiries. Arrived in the capital, he had transacted his business with the utmost despatch, and was on his way back before Desirée could contact him. He landed soon after Rachel was on her way back to Aghios Petros with Cass, thus upsetting Desirée's carefully considered plans. She had no option but to admit that Rachel had gone to collect her belongings, and used Cass's explanation of amnesia to account for her failure to report her survival. Panos was told Rachel had accidentally fallen overboard, and he was furious at the negligence of his crew, for surely someone must have seen or heard her? Nor was he pleased to learn that Caspar Dakers had rescued her. He was familiar with the author's writings about Corfu, and his reputation. He was no fit associate for an innocent young girl, he told Desirée in strong terms, and he would go and fetch her himself, and without allowing her to accompany him, for he was beginning to be suspicious of Desirée's motives and doubted her veracity.

Being a man of action he forthwith hired a speedboat; there were no delays when Simonides required anything, for he knew the island very well and the long rough approach to the village. It would be quicker to go by sea.

He arrived hard upon Dion's heels, and finding the door left ajar, entered the house without even pausing to knock. He seemed to fill the living room with his presence; a big burly man, whose head was covered by a mass of short curls barely touched by grey, surmounting a strong lined face, with pouches below the small alert dark eyes, the head supported upon a thick bull neck. He was wearing white trousers and a well-cut navy blue blazer.

His sudden unexpected appearance had an electrifying effect upon the trio assembled in the room. Rachel's immediate reaction was a desire to flee, and since Panos was standing just within the door, she made a movement towards the french window on to the terrace, only to find her way blocked by Cass, who murmured so low that only she could catch the words :

'Enter one volcano on the point of eruption!'

Dion on her other side was struck with awe by this arrival of a personage he had been taught to regard as a legend who was unlikely ever to come within his orbit. Only Cass was his normal sardonic self and seemed to be enjoying the drama of the situation.

Panos paused to glance round the room, taking in the presence of the two men with an ominous frown. Ignoring them, he advanced upon Rachel and seizing her hand drew her towards him, although she shrank from him in every fibre, and addressed her in heavily accented English.

'My dear child, thank God you safe! But why not tell? We fear you drowned. My crew to blame—I sack the lot.'

There was such genuine concern in the small eyes

that Rachel felt guilty. It flashed into her mind that
Desirée had totally misrepresented him, to frighten her
into acquiescence. Her own dread of the man made
every extravagance seem possible, even the unlikely
threat of incarcerating her until she agreed to marry
him. Now she was sure that in spite of his forbidding
appearance Panos would never force himself upon her;
for one thing he would be too proud. In retrospect her
past terror seemed a little absurd, though it had been
real enough at the time. She was certain that Desirée
would not have revealed the fact that she had deliberately dived into the sea to escape him, and she was
glad of that. Panos did not deserve such a reproach,
but she could not allow innocent men to suffer from
her rash action.

'You mustn't do that,' she said quickly. 'It was nobody's fault but mine. I ... I was careless.'

'You as magnanimous as beautiful,' Panos declared.

'No ... but ...' Rachel looked towards Cass for help.
He, however, had no scruples about sparing the Greek's
feelings.

'Miss Reed is easily swayed by reckless impulses,' he
said drily. 'She jumped overboard in a moment of
panic, but I fancy she has since seen the error of her
ways.'

Panos turned his lowering gaze towards Cass, who
was leaning against the window frame, his hands thrust
into his pockets, his eyes mere slits, apparently prepared to exacerbate events for his own amusement.

'What you mean?' the Greek demanded. 'It was an
accident.'

There was a tense silence while he slowly let his
gaze travel from person to person: Cass mockingly

indifferent, Dion bewildered, Rachel, whose hand he still held, distressed.

'You do this terrible thing?' he accused her. 'I not believe.'

'You shouldn't have told him,' Rachel said to Cass.

Up went the slanted brows. 'I thought you advocated complete honesty,' he returned.

'Then it true?' Panos demanded.

Rachel hung her head, and it was Cass who answered for her.

'Madam her mother threatened her with ungentlemanly reprisals on your part if she continued obdurate,' he explained suavely.

The Greek dropped Rachel's hand and muttered something uncomplimentary about Desirée in his own language. Looking at Rachel reproachfully, he added: 'I not harm you. I only ask be my wife.'

Rachel felt ashamed; she should have appealed to Panos in the first place, told him she could not marry him, but that bear-hug on the deck of the *Nausicaa* had terrified her. She said inadequately:

'I ... I'm sorry.'

Panos looked at her a little wistfully. Her bent golden head drooped like a broken flower, her long lashes shaded her too pale cheeks. He did not like her garb, but he knew trousers were the usual wear among her young countrywomen. He would have dressed her in silk, decked her with jewels, but for once he had met a girl who was not venal. Her graceful attitude expressed penitence but not submission. She had not denied her precipitate action and he had to accept an explanation that was most unpalatable. But women were unpredictable, and she might change her mind. Meanwhile the essential thing was to get her away from her present equivocal situation. He turned towards Cass.

'I thank you for your timely aid, Kyrie Dakers,' he said stiffly. 'But you should have made a report at once.'

Cass shrugged his shoulders.

'An unavoidable oversight, because Miss Reed's adventures had caused her to lose her memory. As soon as she had recovered sufficiently to tell me who she was, I took her to Corfu.'

Panos' face did not reveal whether he had accepted this information, which Desirée had relayed to him. Rachel suspected that he found it inadequate. His disparaging glance was taking in the simple furnishing of the room, so different from the opulent decorations of his yacht, and he exclaimed:

'This no place for her, when she ill.'

'It's perfectly sanitary,' Cass pointed out, 'but I'll return her gladly to more luxurious surroundings, since she must have felt deprived under my poor roof.'

Rachel made an inarticulate sound of disagreement and flashed him a resentful look. At that moment she would have liked to hit him ... hard! He was deliberately making a difficult situation worse with his snide remarks. He knew very well she cared nothing for luxuries, she had just told him she was going to Mrs Stavros, compared with whose primitive accommodation his bungalow was a palace. He met her eyes with smiling unconcern; he was thoroughly enjoying her predicament, it appealed to his perverse humour, and instead of helping her he was waiting to see how she got herself out if it.

'I take you away now,' Panos told her. 'You need a long rest, perhaps psychiatric treatment.'

Rachel quailed at this new threat to her freedom.

Panos must think she was deranged. He had taken his notecase out of his pocket and was staring insolently at Cass.

'You take payment for trouble, yes?' His tone was deliberately insulting.

'No,' Cass returned forcibly. Then with a bland smile, 'The lady has given me ample recompense.'

This time Rachel had to exercise considerable self-control not to strike that derisive jeering face. What would Panos make of a suggestive remark like what he had just said, which could mean anything or nothing? The Greek decided to ignore it.

'You ready? We go now,' he said to her.

'Where?' Rachel asked bluntly.

'To the *Nausicaa*, then to your home ... England.'

For a moment she hesitated. She meant eventually to return to London and this would be an easy way to get there.

' A free passage home,' Cass observed meaningly, as if he had sensed her thought. 'I don't think Mr Simonides will trouble you.'

She was not sure of that; abetted by her mother Panos would quite possibly renew his suit, and she felt she could not bear to be with Desirée again. If thwarted her mother was quite capable of trying to prove that Rachel was irresponsible. Since Cass had abandoned her, her only refuge was with Eileen Stavros, until Panos had left the island.

'I'm sorry, but I'm not coming with you,' she told Panos. 'I've made other arrangements.'

'What arrangements?' Panos scowled at Cass. 'You not stay here. That man no good to reputation.'

Rachel was finding 'that man's' attitude quite intolerable herself, but the truth might sting him out of

it. It would also free her from Panos's attentions for all
time. She said steadily:

'Mr Dakers lied to you. I never had amnesia and he
knew who I was right from the start. I had my passport
with me to prove it, but he didn't report that I'd been
found. I've spent three nights here of my own free will,
and . . .' She paused, aware that the attention of all three
men was riveted upon her, Panos with suspicion, Cass
apprehensive, and Dion uncomprehending. 'Mr Dakers
lived up to his reputation,' she concluded significantly.

She looked eagerly at Cass, hoping she had vindi-
cated herself, for now he would know she had put an
insurmountable barrier between herself and the man he
kept insinuating she still coveted for his wealth. What
she had said was true, but not in its wider implication.
Cass had made a pass at her, but he had not seduced
her; Panos would take it that he had, and he would
never condone such conduct. Surely now Cass would
come to her aid when she most needed it. He had only
to say that they were engaged and the whole situation
would be changed. She would be to a certain degree ex-
onerated, and Panos might even apologise.

But Cass the unpredictable did no such thing, though
he was completely shaken out of his attitude of derisive
detachment.

'Good God, what a lie!' he exclaimed indignantly.
'I'm always ready to accept responsibility for the sins
I have committed, but to be labelled a blackguard for
something I didn't do is beyond a joke. Simonides, I
swear to you I respected that young woman as though
she was my sister.'

Panos grunted in disbelief and Rachel's heart sank,
as she realised that Desirée had destroyed whatever
regard Cass had had for her. He would never forgive

her for being her mother's daughter and he had transferred all his bitterness and resentment against the older woman to her. The delicate seed of mutual esteem and affection which she had been conscious was beginning to sprout between them had been nipped by the frost of fresh disillusionment and had withered and died. He wanted no more to do with her.

But one good thing had emerged from this painful encounter; she had lost her fear of Panos Simonides. She saw him now as no longer a lustful monster, but a slightly pathetic ageing man, who too had had a dream of a loving girl bride with whom he could renew his youth and perhaps found a family. But he could still be dangerous, if not to her, then to Cass.

Bitterness welled up in her at what seemed to her to be Cass's unreasonable attitude. He had judged her so unfairly throughout, and if she could hurt him she would gladly do so. The thought of retaliation caused her eyes to sparkle and brought a delicate flush to her face, and with increased animation she became lovely. But Panos noticed that all her attention was focussed upon the younger man, and since he was wise in the ways of women, it was obvious to him that there was much more between the couple than there should have been if Cass's interest had been merely fraternal. This girl who could look so innocently enticing was frail.

Jealous rage suffused his face with a crimson flush, and lifting his hand he struck Rachel across the face, calling her a name in Greek that made Dion gasp and put a protective arm around her, as she reeled back against him from the force of Panos's blow. The Greek lumbered towards Cass with raised fist, but Cass neatly sidestepped the mad bull rush and administered a punch himself which caused Panos to stagger. He stood breathing hard, glaring at his assailant.

'Come, Mr Simonides,' Cass said evenly. 'A light woman isn't worth fighting over, nor does Miss Reed intend to stop with me, she has found another protector, so we're both losers. I suggest you return to your yacht.'

Panos turned to look at Rachel. She, appalled by what had happened, was clinging to Dion, who held her in his arms, while his wide angry eyes stared in horror at her aggressor. He did not understand what was happening, but the Greek magnate had struck the girl he regarded almost as a sort of goddess, and he was shocked and dismayed. The young couple, he so dark and brown, she so pale and fair, made a charming picture, but not one that appealed to Panos Simonides. Believing from what Cass had said that Dion was Rachel's latest acquisition, he spat.

But the Greek boy was beneath his notice, and it was towards Cass he vented his animosity.

'It not end here,' he said ominously. 'You steal my fiancée, you strike me. It a debt to be repaid.'

A cold hand seemed to close round Rachel's heart, as her resentment against Cass died in the face of what might prove to be real danger. She had never dreamed that Panos might threaten Cass. She had forgotten that the man was a proud, vindictive Greek and between them they had mortally offended him. And it was her rash words that had provoked him. That had not been her intention at all, and at whatever cost she must try to placate the angry man.

She raised her head from Dion's shoulder, disclosing the red marks of Panos's fingers across its pallor.

'But it wasn't Cass's fault,' she cried desperately. 'I stayed of my own free will. I ... I made him keep me, I'd nowhere else to go.'

'Shut up, Rachel,' Cass told her sternly. 'You've done enough harm, you'll only make bad worse.'

Rachel ignored him.

'Please, Panos,' she pleaded. 'Don't blame Cass.'

She cast about in her mind for an argument to deter the Greek. 'If ... if everything comes to light, you won't appear very heroic. I'll say you assaulted me on the yacht ... I'll make sure your name stinks if anything happens to Cass!'

The object of her concern was looking furious.

'Please let me fight my own battles, Rachel,' he commanded.

Panos stood lowering in the midst of them. The flush had died away from his face, but there was an evil glitter in his eyes. Rachel feared her words had made no impression upon him and they had displeased Cass.

'This is my battle too,' she said to him. She again addressed Panos, forcing herself to speak gently and she hoped reasonably.

'Don't let us threaten each other.' Her eyes were wide and supplicating. 'I'm sorry I can't marry you, Panos, it was my mother's idea, not mine. I ... I never encouraged you, did I?' There was no response in the heavy face. 'We aren't really suited at all. I'm sure you'll find someone else.'

A gleam of spite showed in the small eyes. All Rachel's pleading had done was to show him where she was vulnerable.

'It well I find out you bad girl,' he said nastily. 'You have two men here.'

Rachel then realised that she was still supported by Dion's arm, and she hastily moved away. Cass laughed and his mirth was wounding. She flashed at him:

'As for you, you're despicable!'

Panos shrugged his shoulders. 'I tell your mamma I take no man's leavings, and certainly not his.' He glared at Cass. 'I go now, but watch out, Caspar Dakers, you may have fatal accident.'

He marched out of the room with all the dignity he could muster, and Dion ran out on to the terrace to watch his descent of the path to the village.

Panos's final threat had brought all Rachel's fears flooding back, and she turned to him with terror in her eyes.

'Cass, he couldn't ... he wouldn't!'

She knew there were still vendettas in Greece and revenge was embedded in the Grecian character. Panos considered that Cass had insulted him and robbed him of the girl he had meant to marry. He was rich and influential with hordes of henchmen ready to do his bidding—at a price. Cass, alone in his mountain eyrie, would be an easy target for a paid thug. In imagination Rachel could visualise his bleeding body stretched on the matting, knifed by a masked assailant. He was not her favourite person after that last harrowing scene, but her resentment began to fade before this last development. She suddenly knew that she would be desolate if anything happened to him.

But Cass did not seem to be in the least perturbed by Panos's threat. He said lightly :

'A bit of pure Greek melodrama. Excitable people, the Greeks, but I'm surprised at Simonides. You'd expect him to be more civilised.'

'He believed you'd wronged him,' Rachel pointed out, clasping and unclasping her hands nervously. 'Even civilised people act violently under provocation.'

'Which you provided.' He slanted a wicked glance at her. 'A modern Helen of Troy—in trousers.'

'Oh, don't joke about it!'

His levity was rasping her strung nerves. The daily press reported murders nearly every day and for less cause than Panos had.

'Best way to take him,' Cass observed flippantly. 'But honestly, Rachel, you're an impetuous little ass. Why couldn't you let me handle him? He'd have swallowed the amnesia story and your character would have remained unsmirched.'

So much for her brave attempt to put the record straight. She said drearily:

'But he'd have expected me to go back to Corfu with him.'

'You could have told him politely that you'd no mind for matrimony, and were going into retreat in a nunnery in the hills.'

'Oh, you can't be serious!' she cried despairingly, hurt because he had no sympathy for her distress. 'I'd never forgive myself if harm comes to you through me.'

'I don't suppose it will. Simonides was naturally a little annoyed by your rash disclosures, but he'll cool down.'

Rachel wished she could believe that, but she was sure that Panos had meant all he said.

Cass went on: 'Really I'm not worth all this anxiety. Didn't you tell me just now I was despicable?'

Recalling her disappointment when a word from him would have saved her from humiliation, a word he had not spoken, she said witheringly:

'So you are ... sometimes.'

'Thanks for the qualification. I gather that now is one of the sometimes?'

'Definitely, but even so, I don't want your blood on my hands. Couldn't you go to London for a while?'

He looked surprised, then exclaimed:

'Now that's an idea. I'm about due for a visit.'

'Then leave at once,' she cried urgently.

His narrow gaze swept her quizzically, as if her intensity displeased him. Through her agitation Rachel sensed that her reactions were not what he had expected.

'How can I go and leave you with Eileen Stavros?' he asked.

'Your concern for me is a little late,' she said sharply. 'I'll be okay, and I want to be alone. What could you do, anyway? Contact with you would only do me harm after what's happened.' Intent only upon persuading him to flee from possible danger, she did not pause to choose her words. 'Don't you understand, you and I are better apart.'

'Do you really mean that?'

She faltered for a moment, then said firmly: 'I do.'

Cass gave her a long searching look, but her expression did not soften. He shrugged his shoulders.

'That being so, I'll hie me to the lights of London if it'll set your mind at rest. Not because I'm afraid of Simonides, but after all this turmoil I feel the need of distraction.'

'I'm sure you do,' she returned absently.

He looked at his watch.

'Then may I suggest that you start upon your journey? It's a long walk up to Eileen's and you'd better get there before dark.'

Faced with the finality of her departure, Rachel began to feel aggrieved; she was not sure whether she had expected Cass to make further protests, and she had gained her point. He was prepared to leave Corfu. So it was absurd to feel this sense of being abandoned. Cass's

thoughts were already turning towards London, the
bright lights, and no doubt adoring lady friends. He
would forget her as soon as he entered the aircraft that
would take him away from Corfu. That she had been
thrown into a frenzy of anxiety by Panos's threat had
left him unmoved.

Controlling her feelings with an effort, she managed
to say quietly :

'Perhaps you would lend me your rucksack? The case
will be heavy, but I could take what I'll need tonight
and collect the rest later.'

Cass was beginning to look troubled.

'Rachel, are you sure you want to go to Eileen?' he
asked gently. 'I don't think Simonides will bother you
any more if you'd prefer to go to England. If you
haven't enough money I'll lend you your fare, and I'll
arrange for you to stay at a small hotel while you're
waiting for a flight, if you can't get one at once. Eileen's
been brought up tough, but you haven't, you aren't
fit to face conditions there.'

'Then it'll be something of a challenge, won't it?'
Rachel said sweetly. She could not bear the thought of
going to Corfu. Desirée might still be there, and though
Cass's unexpected consideration had touched her she
did not want to be beholden to him. 'I'm tougher than
I look,' she went on, a slightly feverish note creeping
into her voice. 'And I'm sure I'll find peace up there.
I want to get away from everybody and . . .' her voice
rose to a slightly hysterical pitch, 'especially you, whom
I hope I never see again!'

The words were out before she could stop them, but
she had not meant to be so painfully blunt. Cass had
dragged her pride in the dust and she could never

regain her former serenity until she had obliterated his memory.

The man's face went completely blank, a mask concealing his feelings.

'In that case, bon voyage,' he said lightly. 'If you find the life insupportable you can always contact your mother.'

'I ... I didn't mean to be so rude ...' Rachel began, wanting to mitigate her crude utterance, but at that moment Dion came running back into the room to announce that Simonides had departed in his motor boat, giving a graphic description of the way in which the craft had swirled out of the harbour.

'Good riddance,' Cass commented briefly. 'Dion, this lady is going to spend a few days with Kyria Stavros, would you be so good as to carry her case for her?' As the boy looked blank, he repeated his request in Greek.

'She not stay here?' Dion looked his amazement.

'No, she doesn't want to stay here,' Cass confirmed blandly. 'She wants to sample the simple life without distracting ... er ... influences. Perhaps you'd like your hat?' He addressed Rachel politely. 'The sun is still hot on the mountainside. I'll fetch it for you from the car, while you finish your packing.'

He went out of the room and Dion did not conceal his distress.

'Lady, you the *kyrios's* woman,' he said.

'No, I'm not,' Rachel snapped, her nerves on the point of breaking. She recovered herself. 'I won't be a moment, Dion, it's kind of you to come with me.'

She went into the bedroom fighting a sudden rush of tears. She could not bear to let Cass see she had been weeping. It only took a few moments to push her things into the case. Every article was a reminder of the happy morning that now seemed aeons away. If only they had not met Desirée, how different her position would be. She would have told Cass the true story in her own time when he was in an indulgent mood and without Desirée's embroideries.

She came back to find Cass holding the straw hat which he placed with mock ceremony upon her head.

'I hope you find the peace you so desire,' he told her with his usual mocking air. 'If you change your mind, I expect you'll find your mother and Simonides are still in Corfu. She won't give up until he marries some-one else, and he will be staying to organise my demise.'

He knew how Panos's threat had frightened her, and was deliberately baiting her in return for her assertion that she did not want to see him again. Rachel's eyes sparkled balefully, as she retorted:

'I almost wish someone *would* stick a knife into you!'

'What a charming valediction!' He laughed glee-fully. 'I've found your visit most stimulating, Rachel, I might even use you for the heroine of my next novel, but I fear your character would be deemed too improb-able, and the plot too melodramatic. *Adio*, sweetheart.'

Rachel made no reply but hurried into the woodlands to escape his caustic tongue. Dion followed her carry-ing her suitcase with an air of puzzled bewilderment. She did not look back, so she did not know that Cass followed them to a point where the path through the trees ran straight for about half a mile and watched her slight green-clad figure dwindle into the distance with an expression that was neither derisive nor contemp-tuous.

CHAPTER NINE

THE soignée demoiselles who had been Rachel's fellow
pupils at her Swiss finishing school would not have
recognised their mate after a six-week stay at the
Stavros farm. At her request, Eileen had cut Rachel's
hair level with her ears, only as she was no expert it
was not level, hanging in jagged wisps about her neck.
Exposure to all weathers had burned her creamy skin to
a deep tan which had been acquired after a painful
period of burning. Arms, neck and legs were uniformly
brown, for she went bare-legged, wearing only espadrilles. For daily wear Eileen had given her a black dress
that had belonged to one of her daughters, and since
Miss Stavros had been more generously proportioned,
it hung upon Rachel's too-thin body. She girded it about
her waist with the strings of a sackcloth apron. The object of this gear was to save Rachel's better clothes
from daily wear and tear, and since Rachel was hoard-
ing her remaining drachmas for her fare home, and did
not want to buy clothes, she was grateful for the gift.

She had offered to pay Mrs Stavros for her board,
but Eileen had refused to accept anything, saying that
as her guest could not be idle all day, she could help her
with her chores in return for her keep. This Rachel was
only too willing to do, and she learned to milk the goats,
and as she developed a curious affinity with the animals,
this became her daily duty. The day upon which she
obtained a froth upon the milk in her pail, sign of an
efficient milker, she had known a greater satisfaction

than she had felt over any of her achievements at school, for this was an elemental skill and bound up with the preservation of life.

When she had come to the Greco-Irishwoman upon that evening which seemed so long ago, she had simply said:

'I've nowhere to go. Can I stay with you for a while?'

Eileen had surveyed her shrewdly, noticing the signs of strain about her eyes and mouth, and told her:

'It is welcome you are, alannah. Stay as long as you like.'

She asked no questions, for which Rachel was grateful; she wanted to put behind her beyond recall the painful events that had taken place upon that last day in Cass's bungalow.

It was a life that was lived mainly out of doors, for it was still summer and the interior of the small house was cramped. Rachel shared a diminutive bedroom with her hostess, sleeping on a rickety camp bed. Georgios, the son who was still at home, slept in the living room on a sort of shelf affixed to the wall, that was used as a seat by day. They washed in plastic bowls, bought in Corfu, in a shed adjoining the kitchen, and the loo was a hole in the ground, as was usual in country places.

The food was simple and plentiful—coarse bread, goat's cheese, and such fruit as was in season. Eileen concocted a sort of stew of vegetables and bone stock for their midday meal; they rarely had meat, though they often ate fish. Dion kept them supplied with that. The hens that scratched a living round the house supplied them with eggs. They drank milk or wine; Eileen made a variety of rather bitter wines which she fermented in huge stone jars. As Cass had warned Rachel, it was a primitive life, rising and going to bed with the daylight, though there was an oil lamp for winter use. To Rachel it brought solace and gave her plenty of time for reflection and she contrasted it favourably with her mother's frivolous existence, which had always seemed so meaningless. Here life was a struggle to maintain survival.

Dion told them that Cass had gone to England and she received the news with mingled relief and despondency. She was thankful that he was beyond reach of Panos's malice, but he was separated from her by miles of sea and land and would never spare her a thought in his busy life.

There were no books or papers in Eileen's house. News was delivered by word of mouth and was often exaggerated. One of Georgios' friends had a much prized transistor, but all he ever listened to was pop tunes and he rarely brought it to the cottage. Georgios was a handsome youth with his mother's blue eyes in a Grecian face. He was building a separate house for his bride-to-be and considered himself lucky to be able to marry at so young an age. Many men had to wait until their youth was past before they had accumulated enough to dower their sisters and, if she were widowed, provide for their mother also. The Stavros family by dint of hard work and Eileen's small legacy were rich compared with most of their neighbours. She told Rachel with a wry smile:

'It was not easy to make himself work. Greek husbands believe their womenfolk should do all the toil outside and in. But it was prosperity I wanted for us, and so he did his share. God rest his soul, he made me very happy.'

Rachel was introduced to the younger Georgios's fiancée, a shy-eyed gentle girl, and admired the needlework she was doing in preparation for her wedding. Cass was expected to come to that wedding, but by then she would be gone.

She had to go into Corfu periodically to get her passport stamped to permit her to stay on in Corfu. She went in a ramshackle bus and the expedition took up most of the day. She had heard nothing of either Desirée or Panos, though Dion told her that on the day after she had left a beautiful lady had come to see Cass.

'They talk and talk,' he informed her, his English vocabulary had increased quite considerably since she had known him. 'They old friends, and when she go, they kiss and say to meet in England.'

Rachel felt a stab of jealousy. Desirée seemed to be trying to re-establish intimacy with Cass. She had, as far as Rachel knew, no current man, and since his position was now very different from what it was when she had first met him, she might be trying to annex him. He had for her a love-hate feeling that might very easily develop into something closer since in spite of her advancing years, Desirée was still beautiful and attractive. Moreover, she knew how to manage men. Her own feelings for Caspar Dakers had crystallised. She knew now that in spite of his irritating ways, his mockery and cynicism, she was in love with him, hopelessly and yearningly. There were days when she would have given anything to hear his voice again, even if he were upbraiding her. That she had lost him through her own folly was no consolation. If she had not removed his ring, he might have continued with their engagement. But that had only been entered upon on his

part, because he thought she was alone and in need of
protection. He might in any case have repudiated her
when he found she was not, and if they had married,
they would not have been happy, because he had no
love to give her, and might have come to find her own
affection cloying. Thus she tried to comfort herself,
but such reasoning did little to ease the ache in her
heart.

Since Desirée had presumably joined Cass in London, and Panos would have gone back to Athens, Rachel
had no fear of meeting either of them when she went to
Corfu Town. On these occasions she wore the green
linen dress as she wanted to look presentable, but with
her shorn hair and sad eyes she looked very different
from the lighthearted girl who had walked its streets
with Cass. On her last visit she had visited the streets
she had traversed that day, trying to relive that happy
morning, and only succeeded in tormenting herself.

That night she wept in her sleep and Eileen rose to
comfort her.

'It is himself, is it not?' she asked. 'That bad boyo
in Aghios Petros. Don't cry, acushla, he will come
again.'

'He won't,' Rachel sobbed. 'He despises me.'

'It was not contempt I saw in his eyes when you first
called upon me,' Mrs Stavros said confidently.

'That was before he knew who I was.' Rachel sat up
abruptly and pushed her straggling hair out of her
eyes. 'He's always been in love with my mother, Mrs
Stavros, that's why he's never married. He only tol-
erated me because I'm like her.'

'But she must be growing old,' Eileen observed. 'And
he is still young and vigorous. You've youth on your
side, and youth always wins.'

'I wish I could believe that.' Rachel laughed shakily. 'You haven't seen her. She still looks young and she's so poised and polished. She makes me seem naïve and raw, there's no comparison.'

'But she let him down, wasn't that the way of it? She's not true-hearted?'

'I don't think she's got a heart at all.'

'Mr Dakers is no fool,' Eileen remarked enigmatically. 'Go to sleep, mavourneen, and trust in God.'

Next morning Eileen announced that she was going to visit a friend in Aghios Petros. She would ride the donkey and Rachel could look after the place while she was absent. This was an unusual occurrence, but she offered no explanation. Rachel helped her fasten a blanket on the protesting donkey's back, and she went off, sitting sideways and looking far from comfortable. She had learned through the local grapevine that Caspar Dakers was back in residence, but she had not relaid the information to Rachel. She wanted to see the man herself before Dion broadcast the news of his arrival.

Rachel always enjoyed the time shortly after dawn when her duties took her to the goats. On the morning after Mrs Stavros returned from her mysterious errand, she came out with her pails and stool into a grey misty world without a breath of wind, and looked about her appreciatively. The summit of Pantokrator and the Albanian mountains were wreathed in cloud. The line of the sea gleamed a dull pewter and the tops of the trees below her were black in the wan light. Beneath her feet the heather and thyme were heavy with dew. All the earth was hushed and still awaiting the coming of the sun, the rays from which would dissipate the mist and burn up the dew, restoring the island to life and colour. Grape and olive were swelling on vine and boughs, for the harvest was not far distant. The heat of summer was waning and the tourist crowds were thinning as autumn approached.

The goats came to meet her bleating, for they were glad to be relieved of their burden of milk. As she settled down to work, Rachel reflected that it was time she moved on. She could not continue to exist in this limbo of thought and feeling wherein she had lost all track of time. The simple life had been restful and healing, and her associates undemanding, but it was not fair to the Stavros family to continue to impose upon them. As winter drew on they would need all the space their small cottage afforded for their indoor ploys, and Eileen had a right to the privacy of her bedroom. Not that Mrs Stavros had ever hinted that she wished to be rid of her self-invited guest, but that was no excuse for lingering. Moreover, she might not be able to obtain a residential permit to continue in Corfu indefinitely and she was not sure that she wanted one.

With the passing of the languorous heat of summer, she felt a new restlessness stirring within her with the touch of chill in the early morning and evening. She was too young and her brain was too active to be content to vegetate indefinitely. She had been sustained through the past weeks by a subconscious sense of anticipation, as if she were waiting for some important event to happen, but her visit to Corfu, and her talk with Eileen in the night, had forced upon her the knowledge that the thing for which she secretly longed could never come to pass. Cass had gone out of her life, it was no good waiting for him to return to Corfu. If they did meet it would only be as casual acquaintances and would only cause her pain. It would be much wiser to go to some place that had no connection with him, and make herself a new life with no associations with the old. She was strong enough to do it if she set her mind to it, and a job among ordinary people who behaved normally was what she needed. Then she could forget Desirée's treachery, Panos's threats and Cass's rejection. She could never wholly eradicate the impression they had all three made upon her sensitive mind, but she could get them and the events connected with them into perspective, and none of them would have influence upon her future.

Only one more goat waited for her ministrations. Aphrodite was a tiresome animal and contrary. Her name was a misnomer, for she was not a beautiful creature and her character was perverse. She was chewing her cud with rhythmic motions of her jaws as she watched Rachel out of wicked greenish eyes. Black and white, she was a horned variety and had more than once butted Rachel in play or out of maliciousness when least expected and sent her sprawling. Then she would seem to grin with goatish glee and scamper off defying capture. Rachel had become used to her tricks. Leaving her pail and stool at a distance, she sauntered past the goat as if intent upon a distant object. She picked a spray or two of heather, then, when level with Aphrodite, she suddenly lunged and caught hold of the collar around the animal's neck before she could skip aside.

'Got you!' she cried triumphantly.

She dragged the goat to a stake stuck upright in the ground and secured her to it, but when she had fetched her pail and stool, Aphrodite lay down.

'Oh, drat you!' Rachel exclaimed, prodding the beast, but Aphrodite's bulk expressed complete lack of co-operation.

Every drop of milk was precious, especially as several animals had gone dry, expecting the imminent arrival of their kids, or else Rachel would have left the tiresome beast unmilked until such time as she was prepared to submit, but such delay might diminish her supply. She tried to heave her to her feet, but Aphrodite was heavy. She turned her head as far as she was able and the goat's eyes seemed to mock her efforts.

'I'm not surprised you're associated with the devil,' Rachel said in exasperation. 'You're a wicked, evil-looking beast, and if I wasn't so soft-hearted, I'd kick you!'

'*Kalimera, thespoinis,* can I help?'

Rachel became still as stone. Then she slowly straightened herself and pushed a wisp of hair out of her eyes, unable to bring herself to look round. How often in her dreams had she heard that familiar voice with its slightly mocking intonation! As he had spoken in Greek, he could not have recognised her. Her black dress was the normal working peasant's wear, only upon festive occasions did they bring out their beautiful national dresses. For head covering she had adopted the Corfiote habit of wearing a scarf, and instinctively she drew the end of it across her face, as so many of the island girls did in the presence of a strange male, a centuries-old gesture of maidenly modesty.

Aphrodite, recognising the voice of a dominant man, who might be less gentle than the fool of an English girl, obligingly stood up.

'*Efharisto,*' Rachel murmured—she had picked up some Greek during her stay with the Stavros family—and moved her pail and stool. Only then did she dare to look round.

It was Cass sure enough, wearing a polo-necked

black sweater which, with his slanted eyebrows, gave him a faintly satanic look. He was fondling the goat, who seemed to appreciate his attentions. Rachel saw that he looked leaner and browner than she remembered and was even more attractive. She stood hesitating, unwilling to begin operations upon Aphrodite in his presence. Cass glanced towards her and with a motion of his head indicated the now acquiescent goat and said the equivalent of, 'she's all yours.' His lips parted in the charming smile revealing his white teeth that she well remembered and she was filled with a passionate resentment. She had not wanted to meet him again in spite of the urgings of her heart; she knew he could only disturb her hard-won peace.

The wind was rising, dispelling the mist over the mountains and the sea, while the sky flared with the colours of the sunrise. A sudden gust blew Rachel's scarf out behind her head and flattened her shapeless skirt against the shape of her legs. Cass's eyes widened in disbelief and his jaw literally dropped.

'Rachel!' he gasped.

With recognition she regained her self-possession.

'Yes, it's me,' she said briefly. 'Thank you for bringing Aphrodite to her senses. Now I'd better get on with milking her.'

She sat down upon the three-legged stool and with an effort controlled her trembling fingers. She liked milking, finding the action soothing, and mechanically she began to strip the udder. Since neither Dion nor Eileen had mentioned that he was expected, she did not know Cass was back or she might have been more prepared for a possible visit. Presumably he had come to see Eileen and she thought he would go on to the house, but he remained standing by the post to which the goat was tied staring at her blankly as if her appearance and her occupation had stunned him. It would do no harm for him to realise she could be useful as well as ornamental, Rachel reflected, though he did know she could cook. At least he could find no fault with her garb this time; she was well covered except for her bare wrists and ankles. Finally, finding his continued silence oppressive, she said with commendable lightness:

'How are you, Mr Dakers? Did you enjoy your stay in London?'

He did not answer but went on staring at her with something like horror. The breeze ruffled the ends of her hair and rustled in the heather. Suddenly, with a muffled oath, he leaned forward and whipped the scarf from her head.

'Oh, do be careful!' she cried. 'You'll spill the milk.'

'Damn the milk. What the hell have you done to your hair?'

'Cut it off, can't you see? It got in the way and with washing facilities here being what they are, it was difficult to keep it clean.'

'Dion told me you were still here, and I came to ... but I'd no idea ... Good God, Rachel, you look like a tramp!'

'You don't dress up to work on the land,' she retorted, 'and I've been living like a peasant, but there's no need to be so profane about it.'

If she had known he was coming she would have worn something else and tried to smarten her appearance, though there was not much she could have done. Looking at her hands stripping the goat's teats, she noticed how toil-worn they had become; several of her once beautifully kept oval nails were broken. Her hair she knew was a mess, while her clothing was just something to cover her. Cass had come straight from a world of well-groomed, chic women, including Desirée who always looked immaculate, and she must offend his fastidious taste, but she was deriving an odd sort of satisfaction from his dismay. She looked up at him with an urchin grin.

'Nature in the raw,' she told him. 'Now you're seeing the real me without any trimmings.'

'Rachel, why do you do it?'

'I find it restful here,' she said thoughtfully. 'There's no pretence. The people here are as God made them, and though they haven't got any of the things most modern families declare are essential, they seem to be content.'

'So they are, but you're not one of them. Why have you stayed?'

'Perhaps I needed an antidote to Mother's artificiality,' she returned. 'But it's only an interlude. I was thinking only this morning it's time I left and faced the future.' She lifted one hand and touched her hair with milky fingers. 'A good hairdresser will soon put this to rights. These ...' she looked ruefully at her hands, 'will take a little longer. There!' She stood up, hefting her pail. 'Perhaps you'll untie Aphrodite for me.'

'Aphrodite?' he queried, untying the goat.

'Oh, they all have classical names, though in her case I think it's meant ironically. So do the humans—one meets Achilles, Spyridon, and Adonis every other day. But of course you know that, I can't teach you anything about Corfiotes.' She laughed a little self-consciously.

Aphrodite scampered off and Cass moved to take her pail.

'Don't bother with that,' she told him. 'There are no

mock manners here. Women are the toilers and the bearers, they know their place.' She was talking glibly, hardly aware of what she was saying. In every nerve she was conscious of his presence, her heart crying out to him. She had not known how dear he was to her until she saw him again. Every line of his face, every muscle of his body was familiar and precious to her. Yet she must feign indifference, speak impersonally, for she was nothing to him. 'I suppose you've come to visit Mrs Stavros?'

'Eileen can wait,' he declared tersely. 'It's you I've come to see.'

'Me? I'm honoured.'

'Don't be pert, it doesn't suit you. Desirée is anxious about you, I promised her I'd find out what you were doing.'

Rachel's heart sank. For a moment she had hoped he had wanted to see her on his own account. It was difficult for her to believe in Desirée's anxiety, unless she still had hopes of Panos. But his words confirmed her suspicion that he had been in contact with her mother.

'You've been seeing a lot of her?' she asked with pretended carelessness.

'Well, we were both in London. I wanted to know if she'd heard from you.'

'I don't communicate with her,' Rachel said shortly.

'You're very unforgiving. She only wanted what she thought was best for you.'

So Desirée had talked him round and he was prepared to defend her. Desirée could play the tender, anxious mother when it suited her. She did not only act upon the stage.

'That may be,' Rachel said curtly, 'though I doubt it.'

Cass did not know that her mother had been ready to sell her to Panos in return for payment of her debts.

She moved towards the house, and Cass put out a hand to stay her. The touch of his fingers on her arm sent a tremor through her body, and she stared blindly at the frisking goats.

'Wait a minute, Rachel. I want to talk to you.'

'If you're going to try to persuade me to go back to Mother, you can spare your breath. I've done with her sort of life for ever.'

'No, I've no intention of interfering between you and her,' he said quickly. 'It's to do with ... er ... the future, and ...'

'Have you met another Greek girl?' she interrupted, not wanting to hear confirmation of her fears.

'Certainly not, and there never was a Greek girl, as you know very well. I ... er ...' He seemed oddly embarrassed, which was strange for Cass who was always so sure of himself. 'It's ridiculous at my age,' he burst out suddenly. 'I thought I was over all that, I knew too much about women, but during the last two months, I've been forced to realise I've fallen in love.'

'That's nothing to be ashamed of,' Rachel said slowly, though his words had caused a constriction around her heart. 'Age doesn't bring immunity, you know. There've been romances between septuagenarians.' Desperately she sought to keep her words light. 'It's as I said, isn't it, you want someone to share your memories.'

As usual Cass sought to mask his feelings with flippancy.

'That and the prospect of sharing my bed with a golden-haired siren vanquished my bachelor scruples,' he admitted. 'And though we're far from being septuagenarians, we have some good memories, besides the bad ones.'

'And you want to get married?'

'I hope to do so, if she's had a change of heart, and I've reason to believe she has.'

He was looking directly at Rachel now, but she could not meet his eyes, for fear he saw her dismay in hers. Everything pointed to Desirée—shared memories, a change of heart.

'I proposed once,' he went on, 'but ... er ... circumstances intervened. Perhaps I'll be more successful this time.'

Circumstances in the form of a richer suitor, but Desirée was free now, and though Cass was very much her junior, she would overlook that now he was affluent and a success. They had been together in England and his old passion had revived. No wonder he was hesitant and embarrassed after all he had said about her.

'I wish you luck,' Rachel said mechanically. 'Though I don't know why you're telling me all this.'

'But it concerns you.' Again he was looking uncertain. 'Rachel, can't you guess who the lady is?'

'I don't need to guess,' she said dully. 'I know who she is.'

'Then ...' He took a step towards her, his eyes filled with an eager light. He looked almost boyish, being in love had rejuvenated him.

Rachel backed away from him, shaking her head despairingly, wishing he had not told her. She supposed he thought he ought to do so, might even be expecting to effect a reconciliation between her and her mother. A nice cosy little family! But she had rather he wanted to marry anybody other than Desirée, who, she was sure, could never make him happy. Or was she wronging her? Had her mother cherished throughout the years a tenderness for the boy who had adored her and had now become eligible by her standards? She must give her the benefit of the doubt.

Her movement of withdrawal, the lack of response in her face disconcerted Cass. The light died out of his eyes and he looked like a small boy who had been offered a sweetmeat and was given instead nasty physic.

'Could she have been mistaken?' he murmured to himself. But he was not a man to be deterred by a girl's caprice.

'Rachel,' he began determinedly, and advanced upon her, only to draw back with an expression of almost comical dismay.

'You smell of goat!'

'Hardly surprising,' she retorted tartly. 'This is my goatherd's dress and goat smell is most pervasive.'

'I can't bear seeing you like this,' he declared vehemently. 'Let me take you into Corfu, get you properly fitted out and your hair trimmed. You used to be so beautiful.'

As her mother was. Desirée would never appear before any man without being groomed and scented.

'And bathed?' Rachel asked derisively. She was stung by his impulsive words. 'What do you expect? You come upon me without warning soon after dawn without giving me a chance to get to a scent spray, not that they have any here. Sorry about the goat odour, but since you've made a study of Corfiote peasant life, you should be used to it.'

'I'm sorry,' he said contritely. 'I was tactless, but I meant it, Rachel—I mean I want to see you looking as you used to do.'

'Thank you, but I'll go to Corfu in my own time and

make my own arrangements, Mr Dakers.'

She drew herself up proudly and turned her head to-wards the mountain crest. The sun was now well above the horizon and a shaft of light irradiated her figure, bathing her in sudden glory. In spite of what Cass had said, she had never looked more beautiful. The black gown whipped by the wind clung to her body like classic drapery, lending her a fictitious height. Her raised face showed the perfect line of neck and jaw, and the morning sunlight gilded her bare head like a nim-bus. Pain and disillusionment had given depth to her eyes and a new strength to her face. She might have been one of the heroines of Greek tragedy, Andromache going forth to her conqueror's bed leaving her dead son and husband behind her, Antigone begging Creon to allow her brother's burial.

The man watching her drew in a sharp breath. She had grown in grace and dignity during the two months he had been absent. He told her: 'You should never leave Greece. This is your natural habitat, the Garden of the Gods.'

'Unfortunately I must,' she said sadly. 'I'm not a Corfiote. You're being fanciful, Cass, just now you im-plied I looked a freak.' A gleam of mischief crossed her face like a flash of sunlight on a wintry day. 'At least here in the mountains nobody minds the smell of goat.'

'Forgive me, that was an unpardonable reaction.'

'A perfectly natural one. Believe me, I bathe when-ever I can.'

A cloud crossed the sun, and she was no longer a goddess but a weary peasant girl, carrying her bucket of milk.

'Come along and see Mrs Stavros,' she invited.

'Wait a minute, I've something to ask you.' A reason

for the change in her occurred to him. 'Have you met your Adam in this earthly paradise? Is that why you linger in such squalor?'

'I don't find it squalid.' She was quick to defend her surroundings. His question showed her a way to preserve her pride. She would hate him to know that she still yearned for him when he was going to marry Desirée.

'Perhaps I have,' she added.

'A Corfiote?'

'There are only Corfiotes here.'

Remembering that Dion had been attracted to her, he looked at her anxiously.

'But think, Rachel, you're an English girl. Once the first romance is over, can you possibly be happy with a foreigner?'

'Eileen Stavros married a Greek, and she was and is.'

That was irrefutable, but Eileen came of sturdy Irish peasant stock more easily adaptable to the life she had to lead. But Cass knew it was useless to try to reason with Rachel if her mind was set upon some island youth. He sighed.

'You make me feel old.'

'Then feel young again, age is an attitude of mind.'

'Such wisdom in a child,' he scoffed.

'I've grown up, Cass.'

He looked again at her controlled face and the wistful sadness in her eyes, only he did not recognise it as sadness, seeing only a mystery he did not understand.

'I think you have, Rachel.' He seemed to come to some decision, for he said resolutely:

'Please be honest with me, there've been too many deceptions between you and me. I still can't quite believe ...'

But what he did not believe was never to be disclosed, for Eileen had sighted them.

'Cooee, Caspar Dakers!' She came running towards them, holding out both hands. 'Oh, alannah, it is good to see you again! Have you?' she glanced enquiringly at Rachel.

'No,' Cass said shortly, taking her outstretched hands. 'You took a wasted journey, mavourneen.'

Rachel did not heed their words, she walked quickly past them, intent only upon escaping Cass's vicinity. Reaching the house she disposed of her pail of milk, then collected her faded shirt and trousers and went into the wash house. Discarding the black dress, she washed as well as she could in a plastic bowl, then returned to the bedroom. There she brushed her short hair, trying to make it shine, and studied her face in the cracked piece of mirror hanging on the wall. Thin and brown with shadowed eyes, her image stared back at her. Over her shoulder she seemed to see Desirée's face, peach-bloom complexion preserved by art, shining silver-gilt hair, waved and shampooed, blue eyes skilfully made up and about her the aroma of her favourite scents, jasmine and lilies.

'You really can't blame him,' she said to her pictured face.

Going to the door, she saw Cass and Eileen were deep in conversation. Cass would be telling Mrs Stavros about his forthcoming wedding, and she would be dilating about preparations for Georgios' marriage. Aphrodite, perverse creature, was frisking round Cass, having evidently taken a fancy to him.

Eileen would insist upon Cass coming in for refreshment, and Rachel felt she did not want to meet him again, especially if the conversation was still about wed-

dings. She looked over to the blue line of the sea.
Georgios had shown her a path down to a cove some
distance from Aghios Petros where it was safe to bathe,
and it bypassed Cass's bungalow. She had visited it
once or twice, and now, as a result of Cass's remarks,
she had a sudden longing to go down to the sea and
enjoy the fresh tang of salt water on her flesh. She could
never get really clean at the farm. Swiftly she bundled
up a set of fresh underwear, her swimsuit and towel,
cut herself a hunk of bread and cheese and put the col-
lection into a plastic bag. It did not matter how long
she was absent, Georgios or Eileen often did the evening milking. She scrawled on a paper bag, 'Have gone
out, to bathe,' and left it on the table. Eileen was not
illiterate, though confronted with the difficulty of two
languages, she had not passed her skill on to her children. Georgios could barely write his name.

Then as Rachel saw Cass and Eileen move towards
the house, she slipped out of the back door, and ran like
a hare for the shelter of the trees. She did not think
they had noticed her, nor would they care if they did.

Once among the trees she took the left-hand fork
that led directly to the sea, a quicker way than that
which led to Aghios Petros, aware of a lightening of her
heart.

CHAPTER TEN

THE cove was almost entirely surrounded by rocks, a deep inlet pool with a small beach of white sand. As there was no road to it and the outlet to the sea was too narrow for any but the passage of the smallest boat, it was usually deserted, and now with the holiday season over, Rachel knew she was unlikely to encounter anybody. Georgios used it as a private swimming bath and when he introduced her to it, made her promise never to go through to the open sea. Within its confines it was perfectly safe.

Rachel revelled in the warm limpid water which retained the heat of the summer sun and curled smoothly over the sand, for there is practically no tide in the Mediterranean and the wind of the early morning had died away. The sea was blue silk and the sun poured down out of a cloudless azure sky.

For the time being she had ceased to think, giving herself up to the sheer physical pleasure of swimming and floating in the cushiony water, which was so clear she could look through it to the sea bed sprinkled with shells and the myriad small fish dating about.

When reluctantly she came ashore, she dried herself with the coarse towel she had brought with her swimsuit, dressed, rubbed her hair vigorously, spread her swimsuit on a rock to dry, and after eating her bread and cheese, lay down in the shade of a tall rock and fell asleep. When she awoke she saw by the lengthening shadows that it must be late in the afternoon. She stretched and yawned, conscious of physical well-being, and felt reluctant to return to the farm. Though Cass would have been gone long since, Mrs Stavros would want to talk about him and she wanted to forget him if she could.

The sight of a caique making its way towards Aghios Petros made her decide she would return by the harbour. She had never seen the hamlet, as she had no memory of being landed there on the night of her arrival at Corfu. Dion might be on the caique and she would ask him for some fresh fish to take home for supper.

Distances were deceptive in that clear air and she found the hamlet was further than she had thought, and the route entailed much scrambling over rocks which delayed her. She paused where a fresh water stream came down from the heights to rinse the salt from her hair. It dried quickly and its fine mesh sprayed out from her head like an aureole.

The sun was moving towards its setting and she began to wish she had not been so adventurous, but it was as far now to go back as to continue, and the path up through the woods from Aghios Petros had become familiar. She knew there would be a moon and she was not afraid of being molested on the way. There were no bad characters among their small community, and if she could find Dion he might offer to accompany her. She did not know in which cottage he lived, but she expected he would be on the boat.

The caique had reached the jetty by the time she came to the stretch of beach that comprised the village. There were several other boats beached on the strand, but otherwise the place seemed deserted. Rachel was surprised to find it was so small, there was only a scattering of houses set back from the shore, and the little jetty running out to sea to which the caique was being moored. The sky was turning mauve and gold above the treetops, and in one of the cottages further up the hill, a lamp had already been lighted, glowing orange through the uncurtained window.

Rachel looked hopefully towards the caique, but the two men coming off the jetty were unknown to her; they were short and stocky and could not be mistaken for Dion's lithe figure. She turned her attention to the cottages. She was tired and hungry as it was a long time since she had eaten the bread and cheese. She knew the unfailing hospitality of the Greeks; she had only to knock and she would be given refreshment and perhaps a guide. She knew enough of the vernacular now to be able to make herself understood and she could ask for Dion. She knew he lived with his parents and old grandfather, and possessed a younger brother and sister. She marvelled how they could all pack into one of these small abodes.

The cottage nearest to her was surrounded by a low wall covered by creepers enclosing a courtyard filled with sandy dust in which scrawny chickens were scratching. In the stately way of these fowls, the cock was escorting his wives towards their roosting place in a lean-to shed, a lengthy process with much pausing and pecking. The entrance was through an archway of thick blocks of white stone, a relic from a more pretentious building that had once stood behind it, probably a convent. The gate, which did not match the grandeur of the arch, stood open. Rachel slipped inside, and halted abruptly as she heard the scrunch of seaboots on the pebbles behind her. She looked round eagerly, hoping it might be Dion, but it was the two men from the ship and they were coming towards the house. They had not noticed her, for they were too engrossed in their conversation, which seemed to be some sort of argument which they were pursuing with all the excitability of their race, entailing much dramatic gesture. They were a villainous-looking pair, the elder one's head and face covered with thick grey hair amidst which only his jutting nose and small bright eyes were visible. His companion had the black stubble which indicated that he was late with his weekly shave, and his coarse features and little dark eyes looked vicious. He had a red stocking cap on his unkempt black hair and to complete his ruffianly appearance, a knife was stuck in his belt.

Rachel had no wish to encounter this unprepossessing couple, and she stepped behind the arch into a clump of bushes which completely concealed her. She would wait for them to go into the house before trying the next cottage which she hoped would contain more attractive occupants.

To her dismay they stopped just short of the gateway, barring her exit, while the older one proceeded to light his pipe. The younger drew his knife from its sheath and lovingly caressed the blade in a manner that made Rachel shiver. Who were they? she wondered. Fishermen? They had not caught any fish. She had heard tales of smuggling along the coast from Georgios, and it was possible these two were engaged in that nefarious trade, in which case they would not be pleased to find her in the vicinity of their cottage.

Then she caught Cass's name. The older man was saying that Kyrios Dakers had come back and his unexpected return seemed to be necessitating some action upon their part. Rachel crept a little nearer to the edge of the arch as a sudden fearful suspicion darted into her mind. She could only understand a word here and there in their dialogue, and that was ominous.

'Him over the water ... won't wait ... need money ... tonight.' The older man perked his head upwards towards where Cass's bungalow was situated. 'We go ... when dark.'

An icy trickle ran down Rachel's spine. With Cass safe in England and herself secure on the Stavros farm she had forgotten Panos' threat. 'Him over the water' might mean Simonides in Athens waiting ... for what? Cass's return to Corfu and the fatal accident. Greeks never forget an insult, only it would not be an accident, but murder by these paid thugs who needed money.

As if to give point to her terrible supposition, the younger man threw the knife he was holding with accuracy at a tin half buried in the sand. It split the can and he went to retrieve it, laughing at his own skill. Rachel shuddered. Georgios had demonstrated to her the terrible efficiency of throwing knives, which unlike a gun, could kill without making a sound.

The older man expostulated at this display. 'Blunt edge,' he said.

The other spat on the knife and ran his finger down the blade as if to test its sharpness. He looked up with a broad grin.

'Still good,' he indicated, making a stabbing motion in the air. Then he enquired, 'Dion?'

'Kassiope,' the other returned, and Rachel knew that her one friend was absent, perhaps had been purposely sent out of the way.

Then greybeard pointed to the sky and said, 'Later?' The other nodded, and they came in through the archway, almost touching her, and went into the house.

Rachel watched the door close before she crept out of her hiding place. Her lively imagination, stimulated by the men's villainous appearance, had convinced her that they were planning an attack upon Cass. It would be so easy to creep up to the bungalow and hurl that ghastly-looking knife through the window at their unsuspecting victim. Nobody would discover the crime until the morning, if then, for Cass lived alone, by which time they would have returned to 'him across the water,' to report that their errand was accomplished and claim the money they needed.

Rachel sped past the other scattered houses not daring to seek aid, for she did not know friend from foe if Dion was in Kassiope. Nor did she think her Greek was adequate to explain what she had discovered to strangers, and she might be unlucky enough to fall in with someone who was in league with the assassins, who would silence her, and how was she to be sure none of them were? Money, she knew only too well, was a powerful force, corrupting loyalty and friendship. There was only one thing she could do; she must go and warn Cass herself. It would be painful to intrude upon him after the morning's disclosures, and to re-enter the bungalow that held so many memories, but in the face of his danger her feelings were completely unimportant. She had only to close her eyes to see that sinister knife quivering in his back.

She came to a gap in the trees massed behind the hamlet which must be the way up to the bungalow. It was a steep and narrow track and she marvelled that Cass ever got a car up or down it. It became broader when it joined the road to Corfu, which from thence ascended in zig-zags though its surface was rough and unmetalled. But it was familiar ground, she had come this way in the car, so she knew she was on the right route. The swift dusk had fallen, but twilight still lingered in the sky. The men would not come until the dark hour before moonrise, so there would be time for Cass to escape. If he went in his car they would be unable to catch him since they had come by sea. Thus she reasoned as she ploughed along the sandy track which was heavy going, but speed was essential. She had only one thought, the man she loved was in danger. Desirée, her despair and resentment were forgotten. If something happened to Cass the light would go out for ever for her.

Occasionally she paused, listening for heavy footsteps behind her, but there was no sound other than rustlings in the undergrowth where some nocturnal creature was going about its business, or a bird, disturbed by her passage, flapped up into the gathering night.

At last like a beacon ahead of her she saw light streaming through the trees. Cass, with no thought of danger, had not closed the shutters or even drawn the curtains, and the terrace was bathed in radiance from the electricity in the sitting room. Rachel turned off the track which made a detour round to the back of the house, and scrambled through the bushes below the terrace, swarmed up the balustrade and arrived breathless and battered in front of the french window. It was set wide open and she paused to look within.

Cass sat in one of the easy chairs with a glass and decanter by his side; he was not reading or writing, but staring into space. Insects attracted by the light buzzed about him, but he took no heed of them. He looked tired and depressed. Fully illuminated by the light overhead he would be a perfect target for someone outside with a gun ... or a knife.

'Cass!' Rachel called, and stepped inside.

He did not seem surprised to see her.

'So you've come, my little torment,' he remarked affably. He got to his feet and his eyes had a peculiar glitter. With a stab of dismay she realised he was half drunk.

'Come, let me clutch thee,' he declaimed, and lunged towards her. With a swift movement she evaded his groping hands.

'Cass,' she repeated, 'pull yourself together. It's urgent!'

He did not seem to hear her. He was looking ruefully at his outstretched hands. 'Always she eludes me,' he muttered.

Rachel walked into the kitchen, filled a tumbler with water, and returned to the sitting room, to find him stumbling after her. She threw the cold water full in his face. Spluttering, he fumbled for his handkerchief to wipe it off and she saw with relief recognition dawn in his eyes.

'Rachel, it's really you? Not an illusion?'

'Yes, it's me, and I've come ...' Recollection of the danger menacing him caused her to clutch his arm. 'Oh, Cass, I've come to warn you. There are men in the village coming to kill you—I think Panos sent them. You must get away at once.'

He stared at her blankly, water still dripping from his hair. Then he began to laugh.

'Good for Panos! Let 'em come. I can deal with them.'

'Oh, for God's sake!' Rachel loosed her hold of his arm. She was nearly frantic with alarm. 'Don't you realise you're in danger? One of them has got a knife.'

Cass seemed suddenly to sober as he realised her agitation was genuine.

'Most of them have knives,' he remarked. 'Keep them for gutting fish. But where did you see these dangerous fellows?'

She told him what she had seen and heard, and an amused twinkle came into his eyes.

'A bearded ruffian and a knife-throwing thug?' he enquired. 'Arriving in a caique?'

She nodded.

'What were you doing down there?'

'I've been all day on the beach, I came down to swim, then I thought I'd like to take a look at Aghios Petros.'

'You were running away from me?' he accused her sternly.

'I wasn't! You'd come to see Mrs Stavros, and after ... after what you said, I wanted to bathe, but Cass, do something! They'll be coming after dark.'

She glanced apprehensively towards the open window.

'Don't get so worked up, girl, I can cope with them,' he said easily. 'They're not what you think.'

'But I heard ...'

'Never mind that. At least they've sent you running to me. That really does intrigue me. Why should you be in such a fret to save my worthless carcase?'

'Wouldn't anyone be in a fret if they thought a murder was going to be committed?'

'Depends upon who was going to be murdered.'

'Oh, Cass,' she cried desperately, 'do be serious!' In her anxiety she seized his shoulders and shook him. 'You're a sitting target with that light on.'

'We'll soon remedy that,' he told her. He gently loosed her clutching hands and turned the light off.

The open window was only a little lighter than the heavy darkness of the room, she could not see Cass beside her, but she was soon to feel him. His arms closed round her like a vice, and his voice said in her ear:

'Now I've got you at last, and I'm never going to let you go.'

At any other time she would have been thrilled by his embrace, but with every nerve strained to catch the sound of approaching footsteps, it seemed singularly inopportune. Besides, she was suspicious of the reason for this display of amorousness. She struggled to free herself, crying: 'You're drunk!'

'I was, but I'm not now.' He buried his face in her short hair. 'You smell of sea and sun, my nereid. Why were you so off-putting this morning?'

'Cass . . .' A sound outside made her strain away from him. 'Oh God, here they are!'

He listened and they heard the squeak of an opening door, the door of the garage.

'The cheeky beggars!' Cass exclaimed cheerfully. To Rachel's dismay, he flicked on the light, then going through to the kitchen he opened the back door, and picking up a torch, shone it into the darkness.

'Yanni?' he called.

There was a scuffling outside and two shambling figures were caught in the torch's beam. Rachel had only one thought, to stand between Cass and danger. She sprang between him and the two men.

'If you're going to kill him, you'll have to kill me first!' she cried.

As she spoke in English her words were unintelligible to them, but not to Cass. With one strong arm he brushed her aside and began to scold the invaders in forcible Greek. They, to Rachel's surprise, looked completely hangdog, murmuring again and again some sort of apology. Finally at some command from him, they picked up a sack which they had dropped and slouched shamefaced away. Cass went to close the garage door, looking curiously at the key which he found in the lock.

'All over,' he said as he came back to her. 'I'm afraid your desperadoes are only small-time smugglers. Sorry to spoil your drama, but no doubt you'll feel relieved I'm in no danger of becoming a bleeding corpse. Yanni has some underhand dealings with our friends across the water.' He jerked his head in the direction of Albania. 'While I've been away he's been using my garage to conceal the contraband. They didn't expect me home so soon and they were anxious to remove the goods before I saw them. I told them I wouldn't report them this time, but I don't want any trouble with the Customs officers, so it must never happen again.' He looked at the key in his hand. 'I must have left this spare on his boat. I do sometimes go out with him, he's Dion's grandfather, and it was from his caique that I rescued you.'

'Oh!' Rachel began to feel dizzy. She needed food and she had been very frightened. 'And I ran all up that beastly track for nothing!'

Cass was looking at her strangely. 'You really did believe they were coming to do me in, didn't you? And you put yourself between me and them expecting them to throw a knife ... Rachel!'

Rachel had slipped down to the floor a crumpled heap at his feet.

She came to to find herself on Cass's knees in the depths of the armchair encircled by his arm, while he held a glass of spirits to her lips with his free hand. She gulped some of the contents, unable to do otherwise, spluttered and gasped.

'Better?' he asked, and his voice was very soft.

She nodded, and as she had done once before on board the caique snuggled against him.

'Don't let me wake up,' she murmured.

'I'm afraid you'll have to.' He gave her a slight shake. 'From the way you've behaved I would naturally conclude you care quite a lot about me. Why then in God's name did you put on that frozen act when I came up to the farm to ask you to marry me?'

Rachel's eyes flew open and she stared blankly into the narrow grey orbs so near her own.

'You were telling me you were going to marry Mother.'

'What!' This time he did shake her, and not gently. 'Either I'm mad or you are. Marry Desirée? What have I done to deserve such a fate?'

'But you loved her.'

'I never loved her. When I was a callow youth I became infatuated with a being of my own creation who never existed.'

Rachel tried to draw away from him. That might be true, but he had only been attracted to her because she resembled Desirée. And because of that he had believed she was equally mercenary. Perhaps now he was convinced she was not, but she did not want any more protection, she wanted love, and not possible gratitude either, because she had exerted herself to warn him of a danger that had not existed.

'Well, don't make up fantasies about me because I look like her,' she said tartly.

'You don't look like her now,' he returned, frustrating her efforts to free herself and rumpling her hair.

'I suppose this will grow again? I kept expecting you'd arrive in London and I kept in touch with Desirée hoping you would write to her. But you never did, so I came back here to try to trace you, and then last night Eileen came to me and told me you were still with her and fretting for me.'

'Oh!' She buried her face against his shoulder, appalled by this treachery. 'How could she, when you don't want me?'

'Don't I?' A throb of feeling came into his voice as he went on earnestly. 'Listen, Rachel, when I got back to London I found I couldn't forget you. You'd wormed your way into my heart and I couldn't put you out of it. I felt like a boy with his first love. The truth is, my little sea waif, I can't do without you. I want you here always, as my wife.'

She lifted her head. 'Really, Cass, no kidding?'

'I don't kid about serious things. I know I'm a lot older than you ...'

'As if that mattered!' Her eyes were beginning to shine.

'I feared it might. You're so fond of Dion who's nearer your age, and I believed when we parted you wanted to be rid of me. You said you didn't want to see me again and you'd taken off my ring ...'

'The stupidest thing I ever did!'

'It was a trifle misleading and earned you a slap in the face. Incidentally, I ran across Simonides in London and I told him, in a burst of optimism which I feared was unfounded, that I intended to marry you.'

Rachel shrank back against his arm. 'What ... what did he say?'

'That it was time I did, and I quite agree. What do you think?'

'That you're both perfectly right,' she said demurely. With a happy sigh she raised her arms and clasped his neck. 'I do love you, Cass, I think I always have.'

'You'd a funny way of showing it. But you're improving.'

His arms tightened and his lips sought hers. They clung together in wordless ecstasy.

A loud knocking at the back door brought them back to reality.

'Now what?' Cass groaned. 'Can we never be left in peace?' Reluctantly he let her slip from him into the armchair and went to answer the door.

It was Georgios Stavros. Rachel had gone down to the cove to bathe, he told Cass, and had not come back. He had been searching for her, his mother was anxious about her, fearing she might have gone out into the open sea and might be drowned.

Cass began to laugh. 'Come in, boy,' he bade him through his mirth. 'She's safe and sound.' He followed Georgios into the sitting room. 'She's always being supposed to be drowned, and it seems to be my role in life to give her a haven. Only this time she came to rescue me, in more ways than one. Will you congratulate us?'

Georgios looked from the starry-eyed Rachel to the laughing Caspar Dakers.

'Mamma always say it come right,' he said in his halting English. 'We have two weddings, yes?'

'I don't think we can wait until yours,' Cass declared, 'but we'll both dance at it. And that reminds me . . .' He took something out of a box on the table. 'You'd better let me put this on again, darling.'

It was the half-hoop of brilliants.

'The moon's up now,' Georgios told them. 'Are you home to come, Rachel?'

Cass sighed. 'I'm afraid she'd better. Like your countrymen, I prefer an immaculate bride.' His eyes were brimming with mischief. 'But we must have something to eat first, the poor girl's starving, and then I'll walk back with you. Moonlight is so romantic.'

'Romantic . . . you?' Rachel scoffed.

'I'm not too old to learn,' Cass told her. 'And if Georgios will go on ahead, I'll show you just how romantic I can be.'

Remember when a good love story made you feel like holding hands?

The wonder of love is timeless. Once discovered, love remains, despite the passage of time. Harlequin brings you stories of true love, about women the world over—women like you.

Harlequin Romances with the Harlequin magic...

Recapture the sparkle of first love...relive the joy of true romance...enjoy these stories of love today.

Eight new novels every month—wherever paperbacks are sold.

What readers say about Harlequin Romances

"I can't imagine my reading life without Harlequin."

"I get hours of relaxation and enjoyment reading Harlequins."

"I'm really hooked and I love it."

"Harlequins help me to escape from housework into a world of romance, adventure and travel."

"I have never read a Harlequin that I did not like. They are all wonderful books."

"I just want you to know that I enjoy
  Harlequin Romances more than any book
  I have ever read except the Bible."
    L.V., Rossville, Georgia

"I can think of no better way of relaxing
  than with a Harlequin. They allow me to
  face my world with a smile and new
  confidence."
    L.F., Ames, Iowa

"Your books…are just what the doctor
  ordered."
    K.B., Decatur, Georgia

"I just read my first three Harlequins. It is
  Sunday today, otherwise I would go back
  to the bookstore to get some more."
    E.S., Kingston, Ontario

*Names available on request

What readers say about Harlequin Romances

"I feel as if I am in a different world every time I read a Harlequin."
A.T.,* Detroit, Michigan

"Harlequins have been my passport to the world. I have been many places without ever leaving my doorstep."
P.Z., Belvedere, Illinois

"I like Harlequin books because they tell so much about other countries."
N.G., Rouyn, Quebec

"Your books offer a world of knowledge about places and people."
L.J., New Orleans, Louisiana

"Your books turn my...life into something quite exciting."
B.M. Baldwin Park, California

"Harlequins take away the world's troubles and for a while you can live in a world of your own where love reigns supreme."

L.S., Beltsville, Maryland

"Thank you for bringing romance back to me."

J.W., Tehachapi, California

"I find Harlequins are the only stories on the market that give me a satisfying romance with sufficient depth without being maudlin."

C.S., Bangor, Maine

"Harlequins are magic carpets...away from pain and depression...away to other people and other countries one might never know otherwise."

H.R., Akron, Ohio

*Names available on request